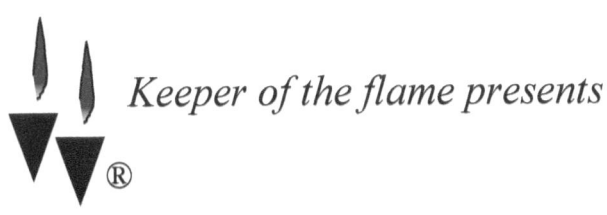

Keeper of the flame presents ®

The House That Jacc Built

Dawn Walker

 ® KEEPER OF THE FLAME

An imprint of Genesis Universal Publishing Conglomerate, LLC

Copyright © 2008 by Dawn Walker
ISBN 978-0-9704171-1-4

First keeper of the flame softcover printing: xxxxxx 2008
10   9   8   7   6   5   4   3   2   1

Dedication:

In memory of my mother, Stephanie Walker Jones, who in my eyes will forever be one of God's Lilies in the Valleys.

Acknowledgement:

In my Father's house are many mansions: if it were not so, I would have told you. I go to prepare a place for you

And if I go and prepare a place for you, I will come again, and receive you unto myself; that where I am, there ye may be also

John 14:2-3

A PLACE

For homeless men, women, and children worldwide

A place to call our own will be our foundation stone
So we no longer have to roam
A place where we belong will be our majestic throne
For healing all the wrong that ultimately made us strong
A place to be at rest after passing the test of living without
In a world of material clout
A place our very own will produce a joyful song that goes on
And on long after we've reached
A place called home

–Jacc –

Prologue ✍

WHERE do the homeless go? This question may never cross your mind until you suddenly find yourself thrust into the vortex of homelessness. It's the predominate question that takes precedence for all who are in the predicament.

Where do the homeless go when they're forced to leave shelters every morning and roam the streets like aimless vagabonds with all their worldly possessions? Thus begins their quest to find somewhere to go. Many homeless people take refuge in fast-food restaurants and hospital waiting areas until they're asked to leave.

Some stand in building doorways and street corners. Many sit on curbs or lollygag in alleys while others try to assimilate into mainstream society by hanging out at public libraries and airports. For those who choose not to tolerate the inhumane treatment that's happening all too often in shelters, they sleep in their cars, on subway trains, in cardboard boxes, on park benches, under highway overpasses, and anywhere they can lay their head.

Again, where do the homeless go? I'll tell you where they go. They go home. Thanks to the homes that are being built in my name, many homeless people have a home of their own to go to. My name is Jacc. This is the story of the house that I built. It's not the famed story derived from the legendary nursery rhyme, but it's the inspirational story of my life as a homeless man and the dream I had. Although I've been dead for over twenty-five years, my legacy lives on through Diane…the woman I love…the woman I left behind. This is our story.

*C*hapter One ✍

ON a scorching summer day in June of 2002, the temperature reached a near hundred degrees. It seemed like we'd been standing in line for hours. People pushed and shoved when the church doors finally opened. A scruffy looking white man with dirty hair and dingy clothes blocked the entrance. He didn't mind flaunting his power as he towered over hundreds of people anxiously waiting to be fed. "Hand me your tickets as you enter! No ticket, no food!"

This was the typical scene at any food line in the surrounding area of Chicago's Uptown. It was hard to believe I'd been on the trail for six months. "On the trail" was homeless jargon for following the food trail. The feeding centers and soup kitchens were the scraps and breadcrumbs you were thrown while on the trail. The homeless also considered themselves to be tramps because they were constantly tramping around looking for a place to eat and sleep. I strongly objected to this term. I may have been homeless, but I wasn't a tramp. By the time the young woman standing in front of me stepped up, the dirty looking man snatched her ticket. "You new round here?"

"Does it matter?" she snapped as she cleverly evaded his question. It was obvious he was being nosy. I laughed as I handed him my ticket and walked in. The woman turned around and I came face-to-face with the most breathtaking creature I'd seen in a long time. She didn't look like your run-of-the-mill homeless woman. Her skin was a smooth midnight black and she wore her hair in long beautiful braids. She looked very exotic.

"What's so funny?" Her almond-shaped eyes were full of anger. I found myself hypnotized by her beauty as I stood like a dumb-found adolescent grasping for something to say. My God, she was gorgeous. She was like a refreshing cool drink on that blazing hot day. "I like the way you handled the old buzzard."

Glad I'd finally found my voice, I wondered what her story was…why was she there? She obviously didn't belong in that arena. I guess the same could be said about me. I didn't fit the stereotypical profile of a homeless man either. I wasn't on drugs nor was I suffering from mental illness and I certainly hadn't fallen prey to alcoholism. I stuck out like a sore thumb in that crowd.

Anyway, who was I to judge? I was now part of the growing statistics of homelessness not only in America, but around the globe as well. I'd recently lost my job and not having a lot of savings in the bank, I found myself being evicted from my one bedroom apartment. Having always been the black sheep in my family, I was also estranged from relatives. What else was new? Homelessness had become a typical way of life in a lot of urban communities.

Dawn Walker

While doing some recent research at the library, I discovered one out of five people were homeless and the numbers were growing. So there I was, Jaccson Ford, young, white, and homeless at the age of thirty-five.

I don't know why I allowed myself to be distracted. I initially intended to find a table before they filled up. In order to be served, you had to be seated and I was hungry. Deciding I'd wasted enough time, I walked toward the tables and scouted around for a seat.

"Hey, Jacc! Over here!" Kango, a foul-mouthed black man with several teeth missing, motioned for me to join him. I didn't particularly like his company, but I didn't see any other seats. Having no choice, I walked over and sat down.

"I saw you talking to Diane. She's one fine bitch. All these niggas round here want her." Kango's filthy mouth was making me sick. I wanted to tell him to shut up, but held my tongue. He was known to be violent and rumor had it he sliced a guy's neck with a pocketknife in an alley one night. The two things Kango lived for was to fight and to smoke crack. I tried to avoid him like the plague. In fact, I basically isolated myself from the crowd. Sometimes it was impossible because most of the men stayed in the same shelter at night and every homeless person in the neighborhood knew where to get a meal. Avoidance was really hard.

Finally a bowl of soup was placed in front of me

from a volunteer server. Talk about literally being a soup kitchen; soup was the only thing the church served. As I reached for some stale bread on the table, I noticed Diane was staring at me. She appeared to be uncomfortable sitting with a bunch of loud and obnoxious people. Kango looked at her table before turning to me. "Why the hell are you looking over there? I know you don't want any shelter bitch. Shit, their ass ain't nothing but whores. All these niggas sweating her like she was all that. You know what she wants, don't you? Tell her you ain't setting out any money for a piece of ass. Every time a new bitch shows up, niggas scope her out to turn her out. Before you know it, they got her ass on the stroll turning tricks. I've seen it happen throughout the years. And you know I've been on the trail a long time. Trust me, these shelter bitches ain't shit!" The filth that spewed out of Kango's mouth made me sick to my stomach. I suddenly lost my appetite. I just wanted to get away, get as far away as possible.

He was right though; I wasn't particularly interested in getting involved with anyone in the shelter. As far as I was concerned, I was just a ship passing through. My situation was temporary. I'd been actively looking for work. Once I found a job, the plan was to save up and find another place to live. It wouldn't take me long to find work because I was marketable or so I thought. The way I figured, I was a victim of circumstances just like many people who found themselves in this situation. The gap between the middle class and the poor was closing at an alarming rate. As time went on, I wouldn't be surprised to see more educated and professional people living in shelters. The economy was the worst it had been in years. Many people had recently been downsized from their jobs. The country was also recovering from the September 11 terrorist attacks. America was in a major economic crisis with poverty at an all-time high.

Not wanting to tolerate Kango's rhetoric any longer, I got up and carried my bowl to the garbage. Emptying it, I gave it to a volunteer. It was only four o'clock. The shelter didn't open until seven. I had three hours to kill. Trying to figure out where I was headed until then, I stepped out into the blazing heat. There was a drop-in center known as "The Joint" in the area. I didn't particularly like going there because of the constant outbreak of fights. The one thing I noticed about the subculture of homelessness was it consisted of a lot of dogmatic people who were prone to intimidation and violence. Unity was a foreign concept. It was every man for himself. I decided to go to the library.

As I sat in the library and surfed the internet, I noticed several security guards eyeing everyone suspiciously. The library was filled with Uptown's homeless. Every day we practically held a convention there. In all honestly, the homeless weren't really welcome; we were simply tolerated. We couldn't be excluded from going inside a public facility. Knowing this, we utilized the place as much as possible.

Needless to say, the guards were cautiously watching to see if they could catch someone sleeping. It was no secret the library administration had successfully found a way to rid the place of us. We were like an infestation of roaches and the library used the guards like a can of Raid to put us out of commission. The guards were their best friends, their ultimate weapon. They were our tormentors, our worst enemies, our harassers. And harass they did. At every chance they could get, they cruised by someone's chair hoping to catch them with their eyes closed. Heaven forbid they should blink. That might be grounds for removal. Under other circumstances, I would have chalked up the guards as just doing their job, but having seen firsthand their nonchalant attitude toward ordinary patrons who dozed off; I knew a different set of rules applied to the homeless. If a homeless person was caught sleeping, they were thrown out.

An ordinary person wouldn't find fault with this policy, but then an ordinary person had a home to go to and a bed to sleep in at night. Sleep deprivation seemed to plague a lot of the homeless. We were deprived of a goodnight's sleep because of the constant bickering in the shelters. For those of us who chose to sleep outside, it was even worse. The hardest thing about being outside is you have to sleep with one eye opened because you just didn't know when someone was going to victimize you. Hate crime against the homeless was always a factor with constant reports of people being beaten while sleeping or set afire not to mention the mentally ill being gun down by the police. Another thing to consider is being chased away from your sleeping spot by some angry person who just couldn't stand the sight of you. When sleeping outdoors, you were always on the lookout for a safe, secure hiding place that would allow you a good night's sleep.

I never understood why society looked down on us? Why were we considered the bottom of someone's shoe? To mainstream we were the social misfits, the lost; we were a disease they wanted to eradicate. Having come from mainstream's working class; the horror of how truly hateful and indifferent people were to the homeless was shocking. When forced to acknowledge the situation, the average person usually dismissed the homeless as an eyesore they definitely didn't want to see.

Was it because if they really thought about it, that man or woman they shunned was once their next-door neighbor, a friend, and even an estranged family member? Surely they didn't honestly believe the homeless suddenly appeared like magic in their communities? They had to know that man or woman they looked down on once had a place to live. Didn't they realize the homeless were once working class citizens just like them? Yes, if they really thought about it, the sad reality is they could also at any given time in their life wind up in the same predicament as the unkempt, dirty, and often smelly man or woman they encountered on the streets. As hard as it may be to face, the average "Joe" is one paycheck away from being homeless himself. The cost of living is increasing while the living wage is stagnated to a minimum. There are many homeless people who in fact work, but can't afford housing.

This is a harsh reality Americans aren't ready to face or accept because we feel we're invincible. We're the land of opportunity, the land of the free. Poverty shouldn't be happening right in our own backyard, nor should it be tolerated. Anyone that doesn't "take the bull by the horn" and make the "American dream" happen for themselves is a loser, a quitter, and just plain lazy. What most Americans fail to realize is it's easier said than done. We simply don't want to believe that forces greater than our own individual efforts have a major impact on our success. We absolutely refuse to adopt this defeatist viewpoint. After all, we're a superpower that's supposed to set the standard for the rest of the world.

Another problem with our thinking is our philosophy has betrayed us time and time again. It certainly has betrayed black Americans throughout the years and now it's starting to betray whites. Although new statistics show both blacks and whites make up a small percentage of the American population, we hold the highest numbers of homelessness in the US. Blacks make up forty-nine percent of the pie, while whites are at a close thirty-five percent. The remaining percent of America's homeless is made up of thirteen percent Hispanic, two percent Native American, and one percent Asian. This is all contributed to the decline in social mobility in the US along with the inequality of income. It seems to me the only thing that appears to be increasing is housing costs, food prices, gas, and the migration of illegal immigrants who'll risk dying to reach American soil. In the recent decade there's been a large surge of illegal aliens. The exploitation of their cheap labor by American companies definitely plays a hand in making sure the government will always "nickel and dime" the minimum wage.

It always amazes me that Americans proclaim two contradictory statements. We scream, "Get a job! Don't be lazy! If you don't work, you don't eat or live!" Then we turn around and say, "Don't get a job at McDonalds, flipping grease burgers, or a job at a factory, a retail store, or any place that pays a low wage. They're unskilled and meaningless jobs, therefore you won't be able to make a decent living. It's a wonder why our priorities are all screwed up. Why we've allowed other nations to come through our back doors and work jobs that are minute, yet vital to our economy. Just ask the thousands of illegal immigrants who come here every day to work for a measly six bucks an hour.

I've always wanted to know who determined that the-forty-hour-a-week laborer in a factory is less important than someone getting paid millions to swing a baseball bat? Why some jobs are considered more important than others? Why is it so important for people to get paid millions to entertain us in movies, on television, through music, and even in sporting events?

If we as a society are supposed to buy into the premise that we must work for our supper, if we're all responsible for pulling our own weight, then every legitimate American who's worked in this country should be rewarded handsomely for their labor. Whether they're a car washer, a garbage worker, toilet cleaner, teacher, doctor, lawyer, entertainer, athlete or whatever, there shouldn't be any pay differential because of the type of labor a man produces from the sweat of his brow. It shouldn't matter if he's white-collar or blue-collar, educated or uneducated, male or female. Every American who works hard should be paid a decent living wage. After all, they're being productive and making a contribution to society as a whole. In my opinion, economists should be suggesting this to congress the next time they're up there on capital hill squabbling about whether to raise minimum wage or not.

The more I thought about it, the angrier I became. America had a long way to go before it would face its own demons. What would it take for us to admit our system of prejudice and class separation is masked behind barriers called education, skin color, and gender? The ugly truth is we like having separation amongst ourselves. We like the feeling that we as individuals are entitled to having more than the next person.

So we created a system that would make everyone strive for an invisible ladder of success, which raises the question of how much sweat, tears, failures, setbacks, rejections, and sheer raw faith does a person need to have before they reach their latter of success? And if they do reach it, will it be because they did it completely on their own or did they get help along the way? These questions may never be answered for many because another sad reality is there will be people who'll strive real hard all their life to reach their plateau of success, but will never make it. They'll go to their grave trying. These thoughts clouded my mind as I exited out of the computer, got up, and left the library. I'd had enough of watching the security guards circle the room. The Joint suddenly seemed more appealing.

I immediately spotted her as I turned the corner and began walking down Broadway Ave. Glad she was walking alone; I broke out in a full sprint to catch up with her.

"Hey, wait up!" As my voice traveled, she stopped and turned around. Delighted that she was waiting, I stopped a few feet away from her to catch my wind. Panting, I bent over and placed my hands on my knees.

"Thanks for waiting," I said between short breaths.

"Was somebody chasing you?" Straightening up, I was once again struck by her beauty. "No."

"Then why in the world were you hollering down the street like an idiot and running as if the devil himself were after you?"

"I wanted to walk with you." She stared at me as if I'd just said something really stupid. "Is that all?" Rolling her eyes, she started walking. Quickening my steps to keep up, I prayed she wasn't going to blow me off. "No, that's not all. I wanted to introduce myself. I'm Ja—"

"I know who you are."

"You do?" Shaking her head, she gave me that don't-be-stupid look again. "What?" I asked wanting to know why I'd warranted that pathetic look. Stopping, she stared at me.

"You're a strange one, Jacc." I like the way her voice sounded. It was soft and feminine. "Don't you know being on the trail and especially in this community, everyone gets to know who everyone is? Of course I know who you are, silly. And I'm sure you know who I am."

She was right. In the subculture of homelessness, you

get to know everyone. Even if you didn't know their birth name, you at least knew their street name. "Yeah, I guess you're right, Diane." She smiled. "You said you wanted to walk with me, so come on." I was glad I was able to make her smile. There was something about her that was refreshingly elegant for the mean streets of Chicago.

"Where are we headed?"

"To the Joint. What's a nice looking white boy like you doing hanging out among the riff-raft? You look like a yuppie. You don't look like you're homeless." Liking her directness, I laughed. "I was going to ask you the same thing."

"Really? You were going to ask me what's a nice looking white boy—"

"N-No. Now who's being silly?" That warranted me another beautiful smile. If she kept it up, she'd have me eating out of the palm of her hands. "I was going to ask you why a beautiful and obvious intelligent woman like yourself is following the homeless trail?"

"I asked you first." She had me there. I didn't really want to go into the full details of why I was homeless. I decided to give her the watered down version of my story.

"Let's see, I was laid off from my job as a cabinet maker after seven years. For a while I lived off my savings which wasn't much. It ran out along with my landlord's patience. After taking me to court, I was evicted. I'll never forget the day I came home and found all of my furniture sitting on the sidewalk. Apparently the County Sheriff's department had paid me a visit. Seeing my things scattered all over the ground hit me like a ton of bricks. The eviction was official. I was now homeless. After the initial shock wore off, I really began to take a long look at the message that was being sent. It screamed at me loud and clear. In this world if you can't pay, then you don't deserve to stay. There is no empathy for personal hardship. The law didn't give a rat's behind about my struggles or me. Every man is expected to pull himself up by his own bootstraps. Somehow if you manage to fall down in the process, then it's your own fault. You didn't try hard enough; therefore you don't deserve the right to live comfortably on this precious soil."

"And your family? Do you have family?" Somehow I knew that would be her next question. "My mom died some time ago. I have a younger brother and my father. I've been distant from them for a while." That was partly true. What I didn't tell her was how much of a distance there really was nor did I tell her my father was the owner of a major building material company. I hadn't seen him or my brother David in thirteen years. I'd completely cut all ties with them. I glanced at her. "Your turn."

She sighed. I got the feeling she'd told her story a hundred times before. "Okay, I've been on the trail for about a year. Like you I was let go from my job. The company decided to relocate oversees. At the time, I moved in with a couple of high school friends. I started looking for work. Nothing was panning out. Then my so-called friends started acting flaky, like they really didn't want me there. Now that I think about it, they weren't really my friends. They were basically fake and phony. I'd finally had enough. I moved out."

"That's too bad."

"Don't sweat it. I learned a long time ago people are only your friends when you're doing well. As soon as you're down, they'll try to find a way to keep you there. Anyway, I did what most would do in a time of need; I turned to my family. At first it was cool, but after awhile they started dropping hints about me getting a job. As if I wasn't trying, yeah, right! I've faxed so many resumes and I've gone on so many job interviews that it isn't funny. The job market is terrible. No one is hiring. Anyway, after a couple of months, I packed my things and left. Being fiercely independent, I no longer wanted to burden them. I was always taught you have to be strong. When I was twelve, an aunt drilled into me only the strong survive and the weak fall to the way side."

As I listened to her, I thought her aunt must be a very formidable woman to have impressed such a harsh reality on a twelve-year-old. Surprisingly, she sounded like my old man. Brilliant in his own right, I often suspected he never really had a childhood. It was as if he instinctively knew he was going to be the head of a major conglomerate from the moment he left my grandmother's womb. Charles H. Ford had always been a no nonsense type of guy with a head for big business. That's where we differed.

Having dropped out of college after my third year, I realized working at some stuffy white-collar job wasn't for me. I've always been a people's person. Brownnosing to climb a corporate ladder wasn't my forte. Throughout my life, I'd seen many of my co-workers strive for upward mobility only to be let go after they'd reached a certain level of management. The notion of starting at the bottom and working your way up may have worked in my parents' generation, but it certainly wasn't working now. In fact, I don't think it's been working for the past forty years. The days of old were long gone. Companies no longer felt responsible for their employees or their communities. They were more concerned with outsmarting their competition. In the process, they've become heartless by scaling back on their workforce. They are also doing a lot of outsourcing and offering only part-time work. It had become immensely hard for a person to climb the latter through sheer hard work and self-promotion.

UNDERSTANDING PAST PAINS

Taking My Own Self-Inventory

How do I let go of my past pain
When it continues to shadow me with its black rain?
When I was a child I felt so thrown away
The feeling of not being loved still haunts me today
I've learned not to lean on anyone
Because if they get too close I'll surely run
From an early age it was instilled in me to be strong
In spite of all the horrible wrong
So I've learned to hide my hurt inside
By building up walls and toughening my pride
My one consolation is I never tried dope
To help me cope
Instead I turned within
And picked up my mighty pen
I write to escape
It allows me to create
Worlds far away
Bringing hope for a better day

— *Diane* —

C*hapter Two*

FINALLY reaching The Joint, we walked in just as a fight was breaking up. The smoked filled room permeated a familiar stench. Once a department store, the center was now being rented by a local social service agency. Filled to its capacity, people sat around swearing and generally being loud and obnoxious. Diane and I had to literally step over bodies sprawled on the floor in drunken slumbers. "Over there!" she yelled against the noise. My eyes quickly scanned the room zeroing in on where she was pointing. Two seats in a far corner beckoned us to fill them.

"Come on." I grabbed her hand and we purposely maneuvered our way through the room. Just as we were about to sit down, a black guy named Malcolm slid into one of the chairs.

"Looks like you're too late, Jaccie, boy. However, if ol' girl wants to sit, she can right here." He patted the other chair. Malcolm tried really hard to earn a reputation equal to Kango's, but when it came down to it, he didn't have the balls to earn the status. I knew he was itching for a fight. He'd tried unsuccessfully throughout the past week to goad me into one. I wasn't going to play the patsy for the little weasel and give him the satisfaction of earning a few brownie points. He could use someone else as his scapegoat. I may not have been on the trail long, but I'd certainly been around the block a few times to recognize what he was up to. Deciding to outsmart him, I took a long sniff and glanced at Diane. "Do you smell that?" Sure enough someone sitting nearby had defecated on them self. I knew I could always count on The Joint to smell of bowel, urine, vomit, and just plain funky body odor. It played perfectly into my plan. Cringing, Diane nodded.

"Phew! It smells like ten-tons-of-get-back!"

Malcolm swore. "Who the fuck shitted on themselves? It doesn't make any sense for these tramps to smell like that!"

"Hey, man," I said, "If I were you, I'd check that chair. It smells like it's coming from around here. Whoever was sitting there might have left a load behind."

"Damn! I think you're right!" Malcolm jumped up. Before he had time to think, I snatched the chair from him just as Diane grabbed the other one. We both plopped down and smiled at Malcolm. His friends started laughing.

"Man, you don't know who you're fucking with. I'll beat you down like a bitch on the street. Get up out of my chair!"

The thunder in his voice could be heard throughout the entire room. People stood up in preparation for the next fight. I heard someone say, "Malcolm, show him you ain't no punk. Hit the white faggot and floor his ass!" Just as he was about to throw the first punch, one of the security guards walked up and grabbed his raised fist.

"All right! That's enough!"

"Tell him to give me my chair!" Malcolm tried to

push past the guard to get at me. Luckily the guard was a large sturdy man. Not that I was afraid of Malcolm. He was puny. I guess the crack he'd smoked throughout the years caused him to shrivel down in size. Besides, I proved my point without feeding into his scheme. Growing impatient with Malcolm, the guard said, "First off, these seats don't belong to anyone, and second, I think you need to take a walk. You're barred from the center for the rest of the week. Now get to stepping."

"Man, how come that white mutha-fucka ain't barred too?"

"Because he ain't causing any commotion. Now move!" The guard began escorting Malcolm out of the center as he shouted he hated all "white devils" and vowed to catch me on the rebound. As everyone settled down and resumed their previous activity, I glanced at Diane. "Sorry about that."

"It wasn't your fault. He got what he deserved. I'm just worried he means what he says about paying you back. Jacc, maybe you should have let it go. We could have found somewhere else to sit." I could see genuine concern in her eyes. She was actually worried about me. It had been a long time since someone had showed an ounce of compassion for me. Since my plight, it had been hard to really find a woman who would understand the situation. Diane was right. You really learn who your friends are in times like these. Suddenly an image of my ex-girlfriend flashed before me. I'd met Heather at my last job. We'd dated steadily for about three years. Our problems began after I was evicted from my apartment. I moved in with her only to learn that she was a control freak. She tried to control every aspect of my life. Not to mention she reminded me every chance she could get that I was living in her home, eating her food, using her toothpaste, sleeping on her sheets, and borrowing her car.

Then there was the situation with her father, Frank. He was a character right out of a Norman Lear sitcom. Archie Bunker didn't hold a candle to him. A diehard republican from a era when unemployment was about three million and the average salary was about $8,600 a year, Frank often referred to blacks as colored, and believe it or not, coons. Blacks were lazy, worthless, criminals in his opinion. He also had strong views about the women's movement. He felt the sexual revolution was the beginning of America's moral decay. In spite of his so-called insight, he was blinded by his daughter's charm. In his opinion, she could do no wrong. She was a pillar of perfection and any man who didn't cater to her every whim might as well be strung up by a tree and hung. Finally reaching my breaking point with Heather, I broke off our relationship. I haven't looked back since. Shaking off my nostalgia, I decided to focus on the beautiful woman sitting next to me. Presently she was engrossed in a news report on the television. A reporter was giving a report about a homeless man who'd recently found a suitcase full of explosives in the subway. As I listened to the reporter give the details, I thought how ironic that homeless people were constantly harassed by the police for riding the subway trains yet this man might have saved the country from another terrorist attack while loitering in the subway.

Diane looked at me. "I think they should give him a reward for turning in the suitcase."

I nodded. "They could at least put him up in a hotel. What he did was very commendable."

"All right, everybody, listen up!" The security guard successfully got our attention by turning off the TV.

"We're closing down early due to a staff meeting!" Groans flooded the room. "You pull this shit every month!" someone yelled.

"Where are we supposed to go?" another cried out.

"The shelter doesn't open for another hour!"

"That's right." The guard's eyes were hard as flint.

"Every month we close for our meeting. Ya'll know the drill. Why are you complaining? Come on, let's go! The Joint is shutting down, now!" Metal chairs scraped the floor as people began getting up. Duffle bags strapped onto shoulders, backpacks hoisted onto backs, and pull luggage dragged across the room as everyone gathered their belongings and began filing out of the building onto the street. "Where to?" I asked Diane as we followed the crowd.

"Let's go stand in front of the shelter," she said once we were outside. "That way we'll be one of the first in line when they open."

"Sounds like a plan." We started walking as the crowd disintegrated and people drifted off. We were silent as we took our time and enjoyed the scenery. It's funny that I'd never run into her before. I wondered how long she'd been staying at the shelter. Deciding to break the silence, I asked, "How long have you been at the shelter?"

"I've been there for two months." She glanced at me. "I noticed you when I first came. You never hang around long. You basically disappear when they put us out in the morning. You usually return just before curfew. I figured you're a loner."

"Aah, that I am. Do you blame me? After all, minding my own business is what I do best."

"N-no, not at all. In fact, I'm a loner too. Besides, there's not a lot of stimulating company to mingle with on this trail. I find a lot of the people are angry and bitter, or happy and complacent with their situation. Most of them are also too busy victimizing each other to really analyze the root to homelessness."

It was my turn to glance at her. I could see she'd given the subject some serious thought. I was curious to hear her view on the issue. Knowing my question would give her the green light, I asked, "What do you think is the real cause of homelessness?"

"Well, if you break it down to the least common denominator, homelessness is an economic problem. Let me also say that it's not caused by mental illness, substance abuse, or any of the other whitewashed-textbook-reasons society is trying to mask as to why people are living on the streets."

At last I'd found someone who saw things as clear as I saw them. Not only was I swept away by her beauty; I was captivated by her keen insight and intellectual mind. I listened as she continued.

"If you take a closer look at the problem, you'll realize people are homeless because they're poor. Poverty is what puts people on the streets. If addiction or alcoholism caused homelessness, then everyone who suffered from these illnesses would be homeless. There are millions of functional substance abusers that are able to maintain housing. Why? They have the monetary means to do so and still have disposable income for boozing and drugging it up. Substance abuse, mental illness, along with the many other stereotypes associated with homelessness is not the cause of the problem. It's merely the reaction to it. The bottom line is there's an unequal distribution of wealth in the world. What humanity needs is a concrete system where all humans can have the necessities they need for survival. Housing, food, and water should be a basic human right. No one should be deprived of them. In this world, they're bought and sold as if they're a luxury that commands a price tag. As long as greed and social separation masked by capitalism exist, you'll always have people who fall through the cracks."

"Diane, you're absolutely right. Homelessness stems from poverty and a lack of affordable housing. The driving force behind it all is a panic stricken capitalist economy that's run by a so-called meritocratic government."

She nodded. "I've never believed in capitalism. It's basically an economic system that serves the interests of the rich by exploiting the poor. I used to believe in meritocracy, but now I don't believe in that either. In fact, I'm not sure what I believe in. What I do know is there's definitely something wrong with the way things are. Take a look around you. What do you see?"

I looked around; noticing familiar faces as people leisurely strolled down the sidewalk while others idly stood around.

Not really sure what she was getting at, I said, "I don't see anything out of the ordinary. Just the same people we see every day."

"That's right. You see the same people who've lived in this neighborhood all of their lives. Most of them lived in these same apartment buildings that have been rehabbed and turned into condominiums. These longtime residents who've patronized local businesses for years have virtually been forced out of their homes by greedy landlords and real estate developers to make room for whom? I'll tell you whom. Condos are primarily built and marketed to people in a certain income bracket. We all know these are the urban young professionals, the go-getters of America. Affordable housing is high on the priority list for them and at the bottom of the totem-pole for anyone else."

"I agree developers aren't targeting the welfare mom with nine kids or the little old lady who lives off a fixed income from her SSI check. Nor are they targeting the just-above-minimum-wage, yet below-poverty-level worker. Yuppies are demanding housing and developers are supplying it."

"True, but it's at the expense of the rest of humanity. It's called monopoly of land and property. What the average person needs is an adequate living wage, not a minimum one. The way things are the majority of the poor will never successfully elevate themselves into the propertied class. The bottom line is it's all about the haves and the have-nots."

"Diane, I've always said we live in a caste system that's more about exclusion than inclusion. Our system consists of several levels of working and non-working categories. Those who don't contribute to the workforce, such as the unemployable, the uneducated, the homeless, and the elderly are basically considered social outcasts. The working class, which is primarily made up of blue and white-collar workers, appears on the surface to be the ideal category. After all, it's the premise for justifying the false notion of achieving the American dream."

"Jacc, when I was young, I used to believe in the American dream. I really believed this country was the land of opportunity, but as I grew older, I began to understand the true dynamics behind our economic system. I realize we're no better than any other society. Our system is not without fault and blemish. Many feel we live in the greatest country in the world, but racial segregation along with lack of affordable housing and employment opportunities keep rearing its ugly head. What's even worse is there's another kind of discrimination that's also emerging. It's reaching far beyond color and gender lines. This new prejudice is against the homeless." As we finally approached the shelter, I thought about Diane's statement. I couldn't help wonder if the stigmas associated with the homeless weren't subconsciously encouraged by social programs and the government's need to classify homelessness as a social problem instead of an economic one. It was certainly food for thought.

The shelter, named Destitution Row, was located in an old landmark building that was once used as a hospital. It accommodated both men and women. Diane and I listened to the chatter as people began forming a line. Being homeless, you learn to adjust to standing in line for just about everything. In fact, you spend most of your time standing in line to eat, receive clothes, toiletries, and to see if there is an available bed for you in a shelter. Sometimes you stand in line for hours in the freezing rain and snow to receive the bare essentials and services. On rare occasion you might find a compassionate person who'll let you inside their facility when the weather is bad. The majority of the time, however, you're left outside until they're ready to open the doors. Such was the case now.

"Hey, Jacc, watch your back around Malcolm. He's a loose cannon." A tall dark-skinned man named Keith walked up to me. Out of all the guys I've met on the trail, Keith was the most unique. A very spiritual man, he was a shining light in the mist of the trail's darkness. Being a God fearing man myself, I understood his strong spiritual connection. We often discussed our faith. "Keith, I'll keep what you said in mind."

The shelter doors suddenly opened. A tall, robust, white woman named Sarah stood in the doorway. "All right! We only have eight new beds available! No pushing or shoving! The regulars come in first!" Diane and I walked in as the line slowly moved. Once inside, the men hurried to their dorm while the women rushed to their designated area. We were all anxious to unload our bags and begin our nightly ritual of showering, eating, and getting ready for bed. Sleep was foremost on everyone's mind since we were awakened at five-thirty every morning and expected to leave the shelter by six-forty-five. I didn't get a chance to see Diane that evening because I was preoccupied with breaking up the latest fight. Life inside Destitution Row was a constant flurry of arguments. Tonight's battle was about a missing blanket. Theft was a big problem. You had to practically walk around with your valuables if you didn't want them to disappear. The staff claimed they didn't have any storage space for our belongings, yet I noticed several empty closets in the building. If the truth were really told, the shelter administrators weren't interested in making things convenient for us. The subliminal message that was constantly being conveyed was we didn't deserve any comforts because we hadn't paid our dues in life. The shelter wasn't our home. We shouldn't expect anything remotely to amenities. It would be sending the wrong message. After all, we might get used to living rent-free.

By the time I successfully diffused the fight, I barely had time for a quick shower. I headed to the mess hall. Sabo, one of the overnight staff, was reciting the house rules as I slid into a chair next to Keith. I don't know why he bothered with the formality. Everyone knew Sabo governed by his own set of rules. A recovering addict and ex-gang member who was once homeless himself, he allowed his inner clique free rein over the shelter. We listened as he droned out his spiel. "For all who are new, these are the rules, and for all who've been here before, this is a reminder. There's no fighting, stealing, drinking, or drug use at D' Row. If you're caught breaking the rules you'll be asked to leave."

"Diane says she'll see you in the morning," Keith whispered. "She decided to skip dinner. Says she was tired."

"Hey, Keith, and your sidekick. There's absolutely no talking while I'm talking. Keep it up and both your asses are out." We glanced at Sabo as he stood scowling at us. It was obvious he enjoyed throwing his weight around. We decided to give him the floor. "As I was saying, there's no sexual contact in here. If you're caught in the act; its grounds for permanent barring. This isn't a motel. If you feel the need for a booty call, I suggest you get off your lazy asses and get your own crib. There's nothing like having your own set of door keys. Lastly, you must, I repeat, you must take a shower. You're sleeping in close quarters in the dorms and no one wants to smell your funky asses. Just a reminder that everyone must be out of the bed by five-forty-five. No exceptions. If we have to tell you twice to get up, you're barred. Now let's welcome our volunteers for tonight. They came all the way from Mount Prospect. They've prepared a fine meal. Give them a hand."

The room resounded with applause as young fresh-faced college students entered the room carrying plates. Everyone began digging in as they set the food before us.

There was plenty and we could rest assure there was going to be seconds. As I devoured the food, I thought about Diane. I said a silent prayer for her. "Hi, mind if I sit here?" A young blond volunteer smiled at me. "No, not at all. Here, have a seat." I pulled out the chair for her. She placed her plate on the table and sat down. "So what's your name?" Instinctively, I braced myself for what was coming. Every time a group of volunteers visits the shelter, we're made to feel like we have to open up and explain why we're homeless. It was almost as if we were expected to perform because they'd volunteered their time. Putting my fork down, I smiled. "It's Jacc, and you?"

"Rebecca. It's nice to meet you. Are you enjoying the meal?"

"Yes, very much."

"Good. How long have you been staying at the shelter?" There it was, the question that usually opened the door to the inquisition. What she really wanted to know was why I was homeless and what was I doing about the situation? I noticed other volunteers attempting to cozy up with several other people. Not really in the mood for another night of twenty-one questions, I sighed as I finished off my lasagna.

"I've been here too long for my liking. What are you taking up in school?"

"Social work."

"Really?"

"Yes."

"Is that why you volunteer at the shelter?"

"Actually, it's part of my internship."

"I see. It'll certainly give you insight about the shelter system. I wish you well in your studies. Too many people are working in jobs they hate just to collect a paycheck. After a while they burn out and become disillusioned. It's takes more than book knowledge to work in social services. First, and foremost, you must have compassion and understanding for the people you service. Second, you should have a zeal for what you do; otherwise you'll end up taking it out on your clients. It's like a person who hates children, yet decides to become an elementary school teacher. Eventually their disdain for the kids is going to reflect in how they interact with them."

"You have a valid point. I'll remember that."

"Good. On that note, I'll say goodnight. It's been a long day and I'm beat. Take care." I got up from the table and tossed my paper plate in the trash. Somehow I got the feeling I'd not only managed to turn the table on Rebecca's little inquisition, but I'd also prompted her to take personal inventory of her career choices. Who knows? I might have saved the homeless population from another cold and indifferent social worker.

SIDELINE WATCHERS

Spectator's Sport For Tongue-Waggers

Standing in the trenches or
Sitting on the benches
Their whispers' carry
As they scoff
Foolishly proclaiming
Persistence never pays off

The sideline watchers
Are compulsive talkers
As well as gawkers

They're constantly projecting negative views
Spreading rumors and lies as if it were informative news
But never disclosing their own personal blues

Skilled in meddling
They sit high up in the bleachers
Cheering failures and giving lame speeches
That has nothing to do with coping
Because they secretly resent those who continue hoping

To one day succeed
Since they'll having nothing to feed

Their appetite for gawking
And undoubtedly talking

After all, they are
The sideline watchers

–Jacc –

Chapter Three

September, 1989 –

"DROP out of school and you won't receive another dime from me. Do you hear me, Jacc? I mean it. I'll cut you off so fast; you won't know what hit you!"

"Dad, those strong-arm tactics may work in the boardroom, but not with me. You can't treat me like one of your business cronies. I won't cow down, not now, not ever."

"Don't force my hand, Jacc."

"Do what you have to. The money doesn't mean a thing to me. It never did."

"Why are you throwing your life away? How far do you think you're going to get without a college degree? I had such high hopes for you. It's always been my dream for you to eventually take the helms once I retire."

"That's just it, Dad. It's been your dream. I've gone as far as I'm going in school. It's not my thing neither is wheeling and dealing in a corporate office. I only enrolled in the university to please you. David can step up to the plate and run the business. It's obvious he's your favorite. I've always been a disappointment to you. I could never measure up to your expectations."

"That isn't true, son, and you know it. Sure, I'm proud of your brother. He has a head for business as I do. You're smart, Jacc. You just need to apply yourself. Even as a child, you were always starting a project to abandon it for something else. I've supported every endeavor you've embarked on only to learn it isn't "your thing." It takes discipline to make it in this world. A man's got to have focus and discipline. Without it he has no purpose."

"I'm not disputing that, but a man has to find his own way. He can't vicariously live through the dreams of his father. Why can't you accept and love me for who I am?"

"If you drop out of school, you're going to regret it for the rest of your life."

"Dad, I've tried it your way. I can't do it anymore. I have to do what's right for me."

"Don't give me that hogwash about doing what's right. At twenty-two, you don't have a clue about what's right. As far as trying, Jacc, you haven't tried hard enough. You never do. What's the use? Maybe if your mother were still alive, she could talk some sense into you. As it stands now, it's hopeless. Sometimes I wish she'd gone through, oh, never mind."

"Gone through with the abortion. That's what you were about to say, isn't it? You wish she'd aborted me. I know all about how you tried to pressure mom into getting *an abortion when she told you she was pregnant. I've known for years. I came home one day and I overheard you and mom arguing. You both were pretty upset and as usual the topic was about me. As I recall, you were on a rampage. It seemed I could do no right in your eyes. You accused mom of being too soft with me. That's when she threw the abortion in your face. I knew it was the truth. I guess I've always known."*

"My God, Jacc, I'm sorry you overheard us. Both your mother and I said things in the heat of anger that we later regretted. We were very young when we married. Money was scarce in those days. We were struggling through college and had decided to wait to start a family. When she told me she was pregnant, I panicked. The responsibility of supporting a child scared me. I was barely keeping a roof over our heads. If I pressured her it was out of fear of failing both of you."

"Thank God your financial portfolio had improved by the time David came along. Otherwise, he might not be the apple of your eye."

"There's no need to attack your brother. You haven't made life easy for yourself or this family."

"You're absolutely right. That's why I've decided to move out. As I've said, I don't want or need anything from you. I basically came to say goodbye."

"Jacc, come back here! We're not through! If you

walk out that door, that's it. I wash my hands of you! Jacc! Jacc! Jaaaaaacccccc!"

I suddenly sat up. I could still hear my father's voice from my troubled sleep. As I ran my hand through my hair, I realized I was perspiring. Throughout the years, I've relived that fateful scene over and over. Each time it's as real as the day it happened. Every detail down to the climatic fight with dad is vividly fresh. I can still see the fury in his eyes. I knew my decision to drop out of school would disappoint him, but I hadn't counted on his enraged reaction. As it stood, our relationship was already strained. Time and time again, we'd battled over everything from politics, sports, religion, to ultimately my future.

Being in exile of my family hasn't been easy. There have been times when I wish could turn back the hands of time and delete that day out of my memory bank. The wheels were set in motion the day I walked out of my father's house. As the days soon turned into months and months into years, I realized God wanted to bring healing to my family, but how? How do you repair more than ten years of hurt and pain? I prayed for an answer.

Needing to take a leak, I got up from the thin blue mat. I glanced at the clock on the wall as I made my way to the washroom. It was approaching two in the morning. Voices could be heard from inside the washroom as I pushed open the door. What I encountered was enough to make anyone sick with disgust. I was absolutely flabbergasted. Two men were engaging in sodomy as several other men including Sabo stood around smoking crack. "What the fuck are you doing up?" he thundered.

"Nature called." I couldn't believe he was acting as if I'd committed a mortal sin when he governed and sanctioned a shelter equivalent to Sodom and Gomorrah. I'd heard that sexual escapes ran rampage in D' Row, but I never believed it. I now know the truth.

"All right, fellows! Clear out! I need to talk to our friend." The two men who were caught screwing had already stumbled out into the hallway. I waited until the room completely emptied out before I relieved myself. Sabo watched as I stood at the urinal.

"Do you mind? If you want to continue the freak show, I suggest you catch up with your crew."

"You know I'm about two seconds from throwing your ass out." Quickly adjusting my boxers, I walked to the sink to wash my hands. If Sabo thought I could be intimidated, he'd better think again. After what I'd just witnessed, he wasn't standing on a leg. I held the trump card. I'm sure the director of the shelter would love to learn he'd not only relapsed with the participants, but he was also sanctioning sexual escapades. "Sabo, you're not in any position to threaten me. I'm sure your boss would love to hear all about what I just witnessed." I could practically see steam coming from his ears as he walked toward me. "If you run off your mouth, I'll make your life a living hell."

"Am I supposed to be scared?" He suddenly shoved me against the wall. "You better be punk! Like I said, you cause problems; I'll make you wish you were never born."
He turned and walked out of the room. I wasn't too worried about Sabo's threat. I knew I had him running scared. Otherwise, he wouldn't have reacted the way he did. Just to be on the safe side, however, I was going to watch my back around him, his crew, and Malcolm as well. As I left the washroom and headed back toward the men's dorm, I wondered how Diane was fairing in the women's dorm. I couldn't wait to see her at breakfast.

It was actually several days later when I finally saw Diane. We ran into each other at a social agency. I immediately noticed her when I walked into the small storefront office. Thrilled to see her, I tapped her on the shoulder as I stood in line behind her. Her brown eyes twinkled with surprise when she turned around. "Hi! It's good to see you. I didn't know you were coming down here this morning."

"It's good to see you too. It seems we've been missing each other in the mornings. Thanks to Sabo, I've had double duty on the morning chores. I thought I'd drop in and get some carfare."

"I noticed Sabo's been sticking it to you. What's that all about?"

"I'll tell you about it later."

"Next!" The receptionist stared impatiently at Diane as she walked up to the desk.

"Hi, I wanted to speak to a case manager about getting carfare for a job interview." The woman sighed as if she was tired of repeating the same old spiel. "I'm sorry we don't provide transportation money or fare cards for jobs. Our budget only allows us to issue them for the welfare office, the doctor's office, and social security." Stunned, I stepped up and stood next Diane. "Did I hear you right? Did you just say you don't give out carfare for jobs?"

"Sir, please step back in line and wait your turn." I was about to tell the woman it was the most ridiculous policy I'd ever heard when Diane glanced at me and shook her head. Turning to the woman, she smiled. "I'm sure my friend is here for the same thing. I don't understand why you give out carfare to go to the doctor's and welfare office, but won't give it out to look for a job?"

"Ma'am, we're allocated only so much money for transportation expenses. We can't give out carfare for every frivolous thing. We just can't afford it." I couldn't hold my tongue any longer. "F-frivolous? Are you saying job hunting is frivolous?"

"Don't be ridiculous. As you know we also offer career development services to the homeless."

"But you don't give out carfare for jobs."

"That's right."

"That makes no sense."

"Look, I've already explained our procedure. If there isn't anything else I can help you with, please step out of line so I can help the next person." I could tell she was thoroughly pissed off with the both of us. I wouldn't be surprised if she didn't have security throw us out on the mere grounds that we were asking too many questions.

"Come on, let's get out of here. It's obvious we aren't going to get any help." I grabbed Diane's hand and we left. The sun was shining and as usual, it was hotter-than-hell outside. Glad to be out in the open air, I smiled at Diane. She looked beautiful with her braids framing her face. Not able to resist, I reached out and touched one.

"Does this take long?" I asked as I twirled the micro plait between my fingers. "Yes, and no. Normally it takes four hours to have my hair professionally done, but I know a lady who does it in half the time. She's not as professional, but she's fast and she does it for free since I can't afford to go to the beauty shop."

Resisting the urge to press her hair against my nose, I let go. "Come on; let's head over to the bookstore. I heard they're giving out free movie passes for next Saturday."

Diane retreated into deep thought as we walked toward the bookstore. Wanting to touch her, I grabbed her hand. "Penny for your thoughts."

"She smiled. "I believe my thoughts are worth more than a penny, but I'll share them with you anyway. I was wondering what we're going to do about the carfare since the agency won't help us? I set up a preliminary interview with a company through a temp service tomorrow."

"Well, we could do like the rest of the homeless population and panhandle." The moment the words left my mouth, I knew I was in for it. Rolling her eyes, Diane let out a loud boisterous laugh. "You've got to be kidding. Please tell me you're kidding. I can't see myself begging someone for a handout."

"Yeah, I know what you mean. It does seem kind of degrading, but what other choice do we have?"

"We could sell that local paper for the homeless."

"You're talking about the Street-Edge newspaper?"

"Yes."

"Not an option."

"Why not?"

"Don't get me wrong, selling the paper can be beneficial, but I've known a few people who've tried it and they were robbed by other street vendors."

"Oh, so what do you suggest? I'm out of ideas."

"How about recycling aluminum cans?"

"And where do you suppose we get the cans? You can't possibly expect us to dumpster dive."

"W-well, sort of, but it's not what you think." I could see that she thought I'd completely lost it. Not sure if I was going to be able to convince her of the idea; I gave it the old college try. "Okay, here's the deal. It's baseball season and there are a lot of beer drinkers in the city, right?"

"Yeah, so, and?"

"Well, when the ball games start, we show up behind the sports bars and collect all the cans the owners will be throwing out before and after the games."

"Is this legal?"

"From what I'm told the bar owners don't seem to mind canners picking cans out of their dumpsters. In fact, they often bring bag loads right to the canners. The police also patrol the alleys in search of any troublemakers who might cause a disturbance and they've never arrested anyone for canning. Trust me; every canner in the city will be there to collect the cans. There's going to be literally thousands of people and you know what that means? Lots of beer drinkers." Diane's eyes lit up with the prospect of all the cans. I could see I'd gotten her attention. Feeling triumphal, I put the final spin on the sales pitch.

"It's the best way for us to come up on some quick cash. All we have to do is show up with a shopping cart, a pair of latex gloves, some plastic bags, and start canning."

"Where do we turn in the cans?"

"At a recycling place Keith told me about."

"It sounds like you've been contemplating this idea for a while."

"Actually it just came to me. I remember Keith told

me he made a bundle collecting cans."

"All right, you've convinced me. I say we try it."

"Are you sure?"

"Absolutely. We need the money and as long as the police are on the scene then I don't foresee any problems."

"Great." Glad we'd settled that, I gently squeezed her hand as we finally approached the bookstore. A line stretching two blocks had formed in front of the store. As we made our way to the back of the line some cranky woman yelled out, "That's right, ya'll better take ya'll asses to the back cause ain't no cuttin the line!"

Diane glanced at me. "Are you sure you really want to be bothered with this crowd?"

"Why not? I'm not going to pass up free movie passes because of some ignorant woman."

"Yeah, I guess you're right." It took some time, but we finally reached the front of the line. We were given one pass that admitted two people. Just as we were about to leave, Keith walked up. "Hey, Jacc, I'm glad you guys made it down here. I hear it's going to be a good movie."

"Yeah, I haven't been to a movie in a long time."

"Me either," Diane added. "It should be a nice treat."

"Jacc, where are you guys headed? I was on my way downtown to the lake."

I turned to Diane. "Want to go?"

"Sure, why not, but how are we going to get there?"

"There's a free trolley that'll take us to the Loop," Keith added. "From there we can walk to the beach."

"Excellent. Keith, you are truly a God sent. Diane can take the trolley tomorrow for her job interview."

"Yeah," she said as we started walking toward the trolley bus stop. "I'm glad we found a solution for tomorrow. I'd sure hate to miss my interview."

No matter how many times I see Lake Michigan, I'm always in awe of its splendor and beauty. We were sitting on the rocks along the beach near Grant Park. As I watched motorboats jet across the rippling water, I felt completely relaxed. I'd heard that water had a calming effect on people, but I think my state of tranquility was partly due to the company I was in. Listening to Diane's soft-spoken voice as she and Keith reminisced about better days was soothing in itself. Deciding to stretch out on the flat surface of the leveled rocks, I closed my eyes. Drifting off to sleep, I suddenly found myself watching a ten-year-old boy standing in his mother's kitchen. *"Look, Mom, I rolled the dough just like you said."*

"That's very good, Jacc. Now you have to place the gingerbread man on the dough and cut out the shape. See, like this."

"Let me try. Let me try."

"Okay, son, you try it."

"Wow! I did it! Mom, I did it! Looks just like a little gingerbread man!"

"Yes, son, you did. Not bad for your first lesson."

"Yep, not bad for my first try. Before you know it, I'll be the best cookie cutter in the world!"

"Whoa! Hold your horses. How about just being the best son a mother could love?"

"What's going on in here?"

"Hi, Charles, I was just showing Jacc how to make cookies."

"Damn it, Shelly. That's not something you should be teaching the boy. What are you trying to do, turn him into some kind of sweet biscuit?"

"Charles!"

"I mean it, Shelly, I won't stand for it. A boy his age shouldn't be dilly-dallying around making cookies. You hear me, son? I don't want you messing around in here with your mother anymore."

"Yes, sir."

"How come you aren't at baseball practice? You should be working on your batting."

"I...uh...I quit the team."

"You what? You quit the team! When?"

"A few days ago. I don't want to play anymore. I'm never gonna to be as good as the rest of the kids."

"Son, how do you know if you don't try? Heck,

you've only been to a few practices. You haven't even given it a chance. Why can't you be like other boys your age? If you spent more time applying yourself then you'd be just as good as any kid. A quitter is a loser and a loser never wins. Is that what you want to be when you grow up, a loser? Because that's what'll happen if you keep throwing in the towel."

"Charles! Now look what you've done. You didn't have to run him off. I won't have you implying he's a loser just because he doesn't want to play baseball anymore. You have to accept him for who he is and let him find his own way. Excuse me, I'm going to go and have a talk with him."

"Jacc, darling, don't be angry at your father. He didn't mean what he said."

"Mom, dad hates me. He thinks I'm a loser. Is there something wrong with me?"

"Of course not, you're young and you're still trying to find your way. There's nothing wrong with trying different things until you find what you like. For instance, football or basketball may be your thing. You have all the time in the world to decide what you like and don't like.

"Mom, if dad didn't mean it, then why is he angry?"

"Son, your father is very competitive. He feels you should always strive for the best. He just wants you to be

successful."

"*Mom, when I grow up, I'm going to make you proud. You watch and see. I'll show you and dad, I'll show you both.*"

"*Son, I'm alrea—*"

"Jacc…come on…Jacc…it's time we headed back." I felt someone tugging on my shirt as I gradually woke up. Sitting up, I rubbed the cobwebs out of my eyes. Still feeling the effects of my dream, I glanced at Diane.

"Wh-what time is it?"

"It's nearly six. If we hurry, we can make the last trolley." Diane had a comical look on her face as she helped me stand. "Gee, Jacc, you must have really been tired. Are you sure you aren't related to Rip Van Winkle? I thought you were going to sleep forever." I jokingly winked at her. "Hey, what can I say? I'm sure the old man's blood must be running through my veins. I could easily have slept for a hundred years." Looking around, I noticed Keith was MIA. "What happened to Keith?"

"He cut out a while ago. He needed to go to his "stash spot" and get some clean clothes." Nodding, I held her hand as we made our way to meet the trolley. I couldn't help but worry about Keith making it back to the shelter in time. Lately Sabo had been on his case about barely getting there when the shelter opened. Apparently a new rule was in affect that required all participants to be in by ten minutes after seven. If they were literally a minute late they were asked to find shelter elsewhere. The fact that we were forced to stash our belongings in bushes and other various places because of the shelter's "no storage" policy was ludicrous. It was especially asinine when they had the space, but were unwilling to accommodate us.

"I see you like cutting it close. One day you ain't gonna be so lucky." As usual Sabo ripped right into Keith when he walked in. Glancing at the clock on the wall, I noticed it was just making ten after seven. Glad he'd made it, I waved to him from across the room. "I hope you enjoyed your nap!" he yelled. "Man, you must have been really tired!"

"Yes, I was!"

Redirecting his attention back to Sabo, Keith grimaced. "I don't know why you're always on my case. I made it in time, didn't I? So what the heck is your beef?" Emphasizing his point, Sabo walked right up to Keith and literally stood nose-to-nose with him. He looked as if he wanted to hit him.

"I've got my eye on you and your sidekick. If you fart too loud you're out of here. Remember, I'm watching you."

"Yeah, well, we're watching you too."

"Is that a threat?"

"No, it's a promise." Having stood his ground, Keith joined Diane and me at the dinner table. Frowning, he sat down. "The guy's out there bad. He thinks he can throw his weight around." I nodded. "He obviously gets off on it."

"Yuck!" Diane looked disgusted as Asha, a stocky black woman, placed a bowl of what appeared to be smashed beans in front of her. A roughneck lesbian, she apparently had a thing for Diane. Turning up my nose, I stared at the bowl being placed in front of me. The meshed nightmare was a sight for sore eyes and it smelled just as bad.

"What the heck is this?"

Completely ignoring me, Asha watched as Diane pushed her bowl away. "What's the matter? You don't like my cooking?"

Diane gave Asha a cold stare. It was obvious they'd had words before. "As a matter of fact, I don't."

"You stuck up bitch. You think you're too good to be here, don't you?"

"I don't think so, I know so. And I also know this shelter shouldn't be allowing the residents to cook in the kitchen. You aren't a licensed cook nor are you qualified to be preparing meals." She picked up the bowl. "Just look at this crap. It smells like a garbage disposal!"

"Bitch, I'll bust your head open so that the white meat shows. You think you're the shit, but you better watch your step round here."

"Ladies, I don't want any problems tonight," Sarah, the overnight staffed walked up. "Asha, go on to the next table if you're through serving this one." Asha gave Diane the meanest look she could muster. "I ain't through with you."

"That woman should learn to smile," Keith commented when she walked off. "It certainly would be an improvement to her looks." Although he was trying to make light of the situation, I couldn't help but worry about her treats to Diane. It seemed like we'd both made some enemies at D'Row.

"How did the job interview go?" It was the following Saturday afternoon. Diane and I were on our way to the movies. "It was a total waste of time. I can't believe I rushed to get there early with resume in hand and dress to impress only to be told the agency had sent another applicant on the assignment the day before."

"You're kidding?"

"No, Jacc, I'm not. The company claimed they needed someone immediately. Since I wasn't able to come in right away, they went with someone else. Oh, well, that's the way it goes. You win some, you lose some." I was glad to see she was taking the disappointment in stride. It didn't really surprise me though. Diane seemed to have a built in mechanism for bouncing back when life threw her a curb ball. Perhaps it was due to her fierce independent nature or maybe it was the fact that she'd been on so many job interviews, her spirits couldn't be dampened. Whatever the reason it was good to see it hadn't gotten her down.

Pleasantly surprised to see there was no line when

we arrived, we handed the movie attendant our ticket and headed inside. As we passed the concession stands, we noticed several long lines had formed. Diane turned to me.

"I see why there wasn't a line outside. Everyone's already here." Grateful we didn't have to be bothered with standing in another line, I nodded. The fact that we didn't have any money was a blessing in disguise. To be honest, I was more than fed up with standing in line for everything we did. Once we entered the dark theater, we maneuvered our way through the rows of seats. "Down there, Jacc." Diane pointed toward two seats. I noticed they were in front of Asha and Malcolm. *That's just great,* I thought. *Two hours sitting in front of them should be fun.*

"Are you sure you want to sit there?" I asked.

"What choice do we have? If we sit up front, we'll practically be starring in the movie!"

"Yeah, I guess you're right. Come on."

"I wish ya'll hurry up and sit ya'll asses down," Asha barked as we slid into the chairs. Ignoring her, we opened our sack lunches and began eating as the movie screen projected the opening segments of the flick. Somehow I knew things were going to eventually come to blows. I didn't know when, but I could feel a storm coming on.

කැකැකැකැකැකැකැ

THE BEGGAR MAN

Ask And You Shall Not Receive

Many won't give a hand
To the man shaking a can
Nor do they really care
As they walk by determined not to stare
Unwilling to stop and pause
They count him as a lost cause

He's just a beggar man not worthy of their time
No, they can't spare a dime!
He stands on the corner everyday
Hoping some spare change will come his way

Hey, what can he say?
He wished things weren't this way
But there's always hope for a brighter day

Until then he's taking it one day at a time
Counting up every thin dime
Praying by the end of the day

When he looks inside his tin cup
He'll have enough to at least get some sup

Then his hustle will be done
Until the rising of the next day's sun

−Diane −

*C*hapter Four

BASEBALL had always been one of Chicago's favorite pastimes and this summer proved to be no different. It was Sunday; the magic and excitement of the upcoming game was in the air as Cubs fans flocked in groves to Wrigley Field to watch their favorite team face off with the San Francisco Giants. Diane and I were standing in the alley of a popular sports bar. We'd decided to get there early and set up our gear before the other canners arrived.

I turned to her. She'd unbraided her hair. Her beautiful brown strands hung on her shoulders. "You look very pretty," I said as I handed her a pair of latex gloves. She smiled. "Thanks. I felt it was time for a new look. So, what do we do now, just stand here and wait for the club owners to start throwing away cans?"

"That's right. They usually start bringing the cans out just before the game starts and then they slack off. They pick up after the game is over and continue to bring them well into the evening."

"Hey, guys!" Keith yelled as he strode up to us. "I see you beat everyone else here."

"Yeah," I said, "it's going to be a good day. There's already a good size crowd and the game hasn't even started." Keith nodded. "I just hope there won't be any drama from the rest of the canners. It can get pretty wild back here. We don't need any trouble."

"Speaking of trouble," Diane pointed toward the entrance of the alley. "Here comes the whole gang now." Yes, indeed, a whole slew of canners equipped with shopping carts, garbage bags, and milk crates suddenly invaded the alley. Leading the pack was Malcolm and Asha. I could tell they weren't happy to see us. Yep, trouble had definitely made its entrance.

"What the fuck do ya'll think you're doing?" Malcolm's eyes flared with anger when they finally reached us. "Looks like they're trying to hold down a spot." Asha rolled her eyes at Diane. I could tell Diane was on the verge of saying something, but held her tongue. I was proud of her for not feeding into Asha's discord. Following her lead, I ignored Malcolm and continued to set up our gear.

"Look, Malcolm, we don't want any trouble," Keith reasoned. "We're all here for the same thing, so let's just make the best of our time and focus on making some money."

Keith's attempt to diffuse the situation worked perfectly. You could almost see the dollars signs registering in Malcolm's eyes. Money was a language everyone understood. "Sho you right, Keith. It's all about the dollars. Just as long as ya'll don't get in the way of my come up, then it's all good."

Diane walked over to me. "How anyone could consider this is a "come up" is beyond me," she whispered.

"Yeah, I know what you mean, but if it keeps the peace, let's just indulge him."

"Sho you right." She winked as we walked over to our cart. Soon everyone was busy setting up things as Marvin's Gaye's What's Going On blared from Kango's boom box.

I was surprised to learn that there was actually a well-organized system in place when it came to canning. Each person took turns receiving a bag of cans when they were brought down from the bar's rooftops. The dumpsters, however, were a free-for-all. And free for all, it was. As soon as the first garbage cans were dragged out and emptied into the dumpsters, canners swarmed in like bees to honey.

The smell of beer permeated the air as arms continuously reached in and out of the dumpsters, bringing up scores of aluminum cans. You would have thought everyone was digging for gold the way they were shouldering each other to gain access into the dumpsters. Realizing Diane and I needed an edge if we were going to stake our claim; I picked up a crate, maneuvered my way into an opening, and scooped up a load of cans.

"Hey! What the fuck do you think you're doing?" someone yelled. "That's cheating!" Ignoring them, I continued to scoop up cans, dumping them into the plastic bags Diane and Keith were holding. "This is a free for all," Keith said.

"They're just mad because you thought of a better

way." Finally exhausting my efforts, I stepped away and let the rest of the canners finish off the remaining cans. This process went on for a while as we continued to receive angry outbursts from everyone who thought we were hogging all the cans. Finally the flow of cans slowed up as the ball game's opening inning started and eager fans suddenly became spectators.

We sat around for the next two hours and just chilled out. The animosity toward us was very strong so we basically kept to ourselves and counted the bags of cans we'd accumulated thus far. Combined with Keith's bags, we totaled up nine bags, which would be about thirty dollars. Not exactly the amount we'd hoped for, but the day was still early and there were definitely more cans to come.

As it turned out, the Cubs beat the Giants winning 8-to-3. Most of the fans were eager to exit the ballpark after the game. Who could blame them? Maneuvering your way through the enormous crowd was challenging. At least we didn't have to worry about the crowd. We were all waiting for cans to be brought down from the rooftops. After what seemed like a fortnight, cans were finally brought down in large bags. Each canner took turns receiving a bag.

Everything was operating smoothly until Malcolm and Asha decided to disrupt the cohesiveness by collecting bags out of turn. Every time a bag of cans was brought down, one of them would run and grab it before the next person was able to get to it. Several other canners started doing the same thing. Diane, Keith, and I were constantly pushed further down the line. Deciding that we weren't going to be forced out of our turn, we headed toward the middle of the alley and waited as bags of cans were brought down.

That's when all hell broke loose. "H-e-e-e-y-y-y-y!" Malcolm ran up to Diane and snatched a bag from her, causing cans to spill out onto the ground.

"Look what you did!" Her angry eyes flared.

"It ain't your fucking turn!"

"You're so full of it! Everyone's jumping ahead of us. When are we going to get our turn?"

"When I say so!"

"Yeah," Asha added. "Everyone here is a regular. They get first dibs on the rooftops. Ya'll have to wait until the regulars get theirs first."

"Who made you the overseer?" Diane glared at her. It was obvious she was fed up with Asha's crap. "Me and Malcolm are holding down this demonstration. What we say goes."

"Oh…yeah…well…we'll see about that."

To everyone's amazement, Diane bent down and started bagging up the spilled cans. I had to give it to her; she had a lot more spunk than they gave her credit for. Furious that her so called authority was blatantly being defied; Asha kicked the bag out of Diane's hands. As I watched the bag sail in the air, I knew it was the straw that broke the camel's back.

No sooner had the cans come crashing down, Diane shoved Asha. Tumbling backwards, she landed flat on her butt.

Before I could blink my eyes, Malcolm swung at me. Grateful for my quick reflex, I managed to duck just as his punch landed in the air. "All right! That's enough!" Two cops came charging at us. "What the hell is going on down here?" One of them asked as he helped Asha up.

"Nothing, officer," she grumbled. "Doesn't look like that to me." His partner stared at me. "Are you homeless?"

"Yes, sir, I am."

"You don't look like you've been out here long."

"No, sir, I haven't."

"That your girl?" He nodded toward Diane as she came and stood by my side. I placed my arm around her shoulder. "Yes, she is." He stared at us a few more minutes before turning to Malcolm. "I don't know what provoked this shenanigans and I don't really care. If another fight breaks out, I'm shutting this whole operation down. I mean it, Malcolm. If I have to come back here one more time today, that's it. Understood?"

"I hear you."

"Good."

"Watch yourself out here," the officer's partner said before they left. "These guys can be real cutthroats when it comes to canning." Although the tension remained high for the rest of the evening everyone kept their tempers under check. They basically ignored us as we continued to rack up on the cans. By the end of the night, we totaled up seventy-two large trash bags, which amounted to $180.00. As we looked for a safe place to stash the cans, I thought about the cop's warning. Cutthroat was an understatement as far as I was concerned. The sooner we hid the cans in a safe place, the better. I knew they were waiting like vultures to steal them from us.

"Hey, man, I know a really good place to hide them until we're able to turn them in. Come on, follow me." Keith led the way as Diane and I pushed the carts.

It took a while, but we finally reached a secluded alley off of an abandoned railroad track.

"Wow! This is really hidden." Diane looked around as Keith and I stashed the bags in a rundown shed. "Yeah, I used to play back here when I was a kid. I hung out with a lot of the old timers. Still come here when I want to find a piece of mind."

"I just hope no one finds our stash," I said as I hauled the last bag into the shed and closed the door. Keith smiled as he pulled a heavy chain and lock from his backpack. "Even if anyone does snoop around the shed, they're going to have a heck of a time getting in."

"Yeah, I guess you're right. Besides, it's only for a night. I say we turn the cans in first thing in the morning."

"Sounds like a plan to me," Keith affirmed as he

secured the shed with the lock and chain. "Come on, we better get going before we miss our curfew."

Rushing back, we made it just in time. Deciding to skip dinner, we took our showers and went straight to bed. No one said anything, but I think we were all anxious for the morning to come so we could collect our loot from the cans.

"Jacc! Jacc! Wake up, Jacc!" Turning over, my eyelids fluttered before they finally popped opened. Keith was kneeling beside me looking traumatized. Alarmed, I sat up.

"Wh-what's wrong? What's going on?"

"Man, something's going down in the women's dorm. I hear it's really bad." Scrambling to get up, I reached for my jeans and slipped them on. Wasting no time, I ran as fast I could to the women's dorm. All I kept thinking was dear God don't let anything have happened to Diane.

A crowd had formed in the entrance of the women's dorm. Profuse wailing resounded throughout the hallway. I instinctively knew it was her. My heart raced as I pressed my way in. "Excuse me! Let me through! Let me through, damn it! Oh...my...God! Diane!" It was the most shocking thing I'd ever seen. Diane was practically bald with only patches of hair remaining on her head. Tears were streaming down her face as she sat on the floor and clutched what appeared to be most of her beautiful long hair. "Whhhhyyyyy…wwwhhhhhy? My God,…whhhhhhyyyy?"

She repeatedly cried. Stunned, my heart felt as if it had shattered into a thousand pieces. When the realization of what I can only imagine to be the most horrendous thing to ever happen to a woman penetrated itself, my eyes began to water. The shock and pain singed my soul. I knew those treacherous, jealous, vultures had done this to Diane. They've always had it in for her. They wanted to destroy her. They also wanted to even the score from today's disagreement at the ball game. It looked as if they'd succeeded.

I turned to the crowd. By now my tears were flowing as strong as Diane's.

"Who the hell did this? Answer me! I want to know what low life did this to hhhhherrrrrrrrr!!!"

As I scanned the crowd, my eyes caught Asha giggling with her cronies. Furious beyond reason, I completely lost it.

"You think this is funny? I'll show what's funny!" As I started toward her, Malcolm interceded. "Touch her and your ass is mine!"

"Do you see what she and her friends did?" Sparks flew from Asha's eyes. "How do you know it was us? For all you know it could have been a bad hair-relaxer. You have no proof so back the fuck off!"

"Yeah!" one of Asha's posses yelled. "The heifer was walking round here like she was all that. Look at her now. It's not our fault the bitch is baldheaded!" As they burst out laughing, I sprang into action. "Jacc, no!" Diane hysterically screamed as Malcolm threw the first punch. He landed a good blow to my face. My anger was suddenly infused beyond sanity. It literally took three guys to pull me off him as I began beating the dog crap out of him. "Ford!" Sabo thundered. "You're definitely out of here along with that broad and your sidekick. Now get your shit and get the fuck out before I have all ya'll asses thrown in jail! "

"Fine!" Keith roared. "We'll be glad to finally leave this ungodly place!" He suddenly ran to the men's dorm and gathered our things as Diane and I scrambled to collect hers. Returning a few minutes later, Keith offered Diane his favorite baseball cap.

"Here, put this on," It was obvious she was still in shock as she fumbled with it. I noticed she was trembling all over as I helped her with the cap. I decided to take her in my arms. I'm not sure how long we stood locked in the hug. It could have been a second, five minutes, maybe longer. All I know is she needed me and I desperately wanted to be there for her. "Diane," I said when we reluctantly pulled out of the embrace. Holding her head down in shame, she avoided looking at me. Needing to reassure her everything was going to be all right, I gently tilted her chin, forcing her head up. "Diane, look at me." The moment her frighten eyes locked with my brown ones; our souls connected on a higher spiritual level. "There's no need to be ashamed. What happened was evil and vicious. It doesn't change a thing. You are and will always be a very beautiful woman. We're going to get through this. We just have to get out of here." Reaching down, I let my lips taste the salty tear that started cascading down her cheek.

"Diane, I love you."

A sobbed escaped her lips. "Jacc, I love you too." Not able to resist, I gathered her back in my arms and pressed my lips to her inviting ones. As we once again became caught up in the moment, I couldn't help think this wasn't how I envisioned our first kiss. Never in a million years would I have imagined we'd finally come to together under these circumstances.

"Ain't love just fucking grand? I don't believe this shit. You got two seconds before I call the police!" I started to say something to Sabo, but thought better of it. We pulled out of each other's arms, grabbed our bags, and headed for the main exist. Malcolm was dead on our trail as we made our way to the front door.

"That's right, cracker boy, your ass is out of here. You better leave town. If I catch you on the street, you won't live to celebrate your next birthday. Diane, it's too bad you turned out to be a hunky-loving ho." Stopping dead in my tracks, I balled my fist when Keith grabbed my arm. "Let it go, Jacc, just let it go. He isn't worth it. Let's get out of here before the cops show up."

It took all of my will power not to let Malcolm have it. Taking Diane's hand, I led us outside. Cool gusty wind blew all around us as we started walking. Diane was shivering. Taking off my jacket, I placed it over her shoulders.

"Thanks." She uttered. "I didn't get a chance to grab mine in all of the confusion." Reaching out, I touched her cheek as we stopped at an intersection. "If need be, I'll give you the shirt off my back."

"You'd better keep your shirt on," Keith said. "I'm not riding the train with you half naked. If we hurry, we can catch my friend before he gets off work. He might let us ride free since he works for the transit system." Upon hearing that we might be able to get a free ride, we crossed the street and hurried to the train station. Keith's friend was just leaving as we walked up.

"Hey, Keith, what's happening, man?"

"Nothing much, I was just kicked out of the shelter."

"Say, w-h-a-a-a-a-t? How do you get evicted from a homeless shelter when you're already homeless?"

"I know, man, it sounds crazy, doesn't it? Say, do you think you can put us on the train?"

"Sure. They were evicted, too? Even the female?"

"Yeah."

"That place doesn't give a damn about anybody."

"Tony, if I told you what really went down in there, you wouldn't believe me. Man, thanks for looking out for us."

"No problem." Using his employee pass, he let us walk through the turnstile. As we rode up the escalator to the train platform, I glanced at a clock on a nearby wall. It was approaching three in the morning. With the exception of a few partygoers, the platform was deserted. Diane glanced around.

"Jacc, do you think it's safe for us to ride the trains all night? I hear a lot of crime happens on them."

"Don't worry. We'll be okay. There'll be too many people riding the trains for something to happen. We'll take this one downtown and board the one that goes to the airport. Then we'll ride back and forth until it turns daylight. By then, it'll be time for us to turn in the cans."

I could see she wasn't totally convinced as she took a few minutes to evaluate our options. "I guess you're right," she finally said when she realized there weren't many choices to choose from. It was late and we didn't have any blankets for camping out.

Hoisting his backpack on his back, Keith yelled against the loud rumbling train as it approached. "Try to find a cubbyhole seat!"

The commuter train finally stopped at the platform and the doors opened. As we walked through the four adjoining railcars in search of a cubbyhole, I noticed there were a lot of homeless people sleeping on the trains. Every cubbyhole was taken. Apparently it was a popular choice because the seats were usually found at the back of the cars and they allowed a certain amount of privacy due to the glass partition that divided them from the other seats. Realizing we weren't going to find any available cubbyholes, we searched for alternative seating. Finally settling on the last car, we unloaded our gear and plopped down in the vinyl seats near the door. Feeling it was safer, I let Diane sit in the inside seat.

Keith chose to sit behind us. "I say we get some shuteye," he said as he pulled the hood of his jacket over his head to block out the train's light. Leaning my head on Diane's shoulder, I closed my eyes and focused on the rapid motion of the speeding train.

"Oooouch! Hey, man, let go!"

"Don't even think about it! I suggest you ease your hand out of his pocket!" I woke up and found Keith holding a man in a chokehold as he slid his hand out of my pocket.

"Keith, what happened?"

"Jacc, it's okay. This stud was just getting off the train, right?"

"Ouch! Yeah, man. Be easy. I'm going." Just as the train pulled into the next station and its doors opened, Keith shoved the guy out onto the platform. "Choose your victims more carefully the next time you try to rob them!" I could see the man scrambling to get up as the train pulled off and began speeding down its track.

"W-What's going on?" Diane sleepily rubbed her eyes as she woke up."

"I just kicked some stub off the train. He was about to rob Jacc when I woke up and caught him."

"My God, Jacc, are you okay? I knew we shouldn't have tried to sleep on this train. It's dangerous."

"I'm okay, Diane. Trust me. Everything's fine."

"Yeah, Diane," Keith added. "It's all good. I took care of the creep. Here's what I propose. For now on, Jacc and I will take turns watching out while you sleep. Don't worry, it'll be cool, trust me." The look Diane gave Keith said it all. I knew she didn't want to continue to ride the trains. To be honest, who could blame her? From what had just transpired, I was also starting to have qualms about riding them.

Just as Diane was about to protest the train pulled into our stop. We quickly grabbed our things and rushed off before the doors closed. "Man, that was a close call," Keith said as we walked down the subway stairs. "I know you guys are a little spooked about riding, but it'll be okay. I used to ride the trains all the time." Glancing at Diane, I winked to reassure her. Silently, however, I prayed for protection. I knew we were going to need it.

To my amazement nothing else happened as we repeatedly rode from one end of the line to the next. Keith and I diligently took turns with the watch duty while Diane slept. What was even more amazing was how quickly time went by. Even though the ride both ways took about an hour and a half, it felt like we hadn't really gone anywhere.

Every time we reached the end of the line, we had to get off the train and wait for the next one going back to pull out. I felt like I'd only slept for twenty minutes. Having our sleep constantly interrupted was an obvious ploy from the transit system. It was their way of discouraging the homeless from riding the trains all night. They didn't want us riding them, but they didn't have a legal way of stopping us because for the most part we were paying customers. As we walked through one cold rail car to the next, I realized they were also trying to freeze us off the trains. Why else would they have the air conditioning on full blast in the wee hours of the morning? Everyone knows its cooler outside at that time. The sun wasn't even out and the temperature certainly didn't warrant the air to be on so high. Yep, it was just another subliminal way for them to discriminate against us.

Daylight finally flooded the sky as rush hour started. The train began filling up with its Monday morning commuters. Deciding it would be our last run on the train, I let Keith and Diane sleep until we reached our stop on the north side. I wanted to collect our cans as soon as possible. "Hey, guys, wake up. This is our stop." After several shakes, I managed to rouse Keith and Diane. "What time is it?" she asked as she rubbed her sleep hazed eyes. "It's almost six." Grabbing his bag, Keith got up.

We stepped off the train when it stopped and raced down the platform stairs.

Cashing in the cans didn't take any time at all. Relieved to find our cans still locked in the shed, we quickly loaded them back into the carts and wheeled them over to the recycling place. "Twenty…forty...sixty." Keith swiftly counted out everyone's share of the money as we left the recycling place. "So what are y'all going to do with your bread?"

"I was thinking we'd find a fleabag hotel and get off the streets for a couple of days until we figure out a viable plan."

Diane shook her head. "N-no way. I don't want to stay in some roach infested, crack haven. I've stayed in a few and they're almost as bad as the shelter. I'd rather take my chances on the streets, thank you very much." After her ordeal last night, I knew she needed to feel safe and out of harm's way. "I guess you're right. We might be safer out here. So, Keith, what are you going to do with your money?"

"I'm going to hold on to it for as long as I can. Spend only what is absolutely necessary. Say, I know where we can lay our heads tonight."

"*Where*?" Diane and I asked in unison. I was hoping he had a better idea than sleeping on the trains. I just couldn't handle another night on the rails. "A couple of old timers told me about how they used to sneak into the back of a U-Haul truck. Although the trucks are cold at night, they're usually equipped with throw rugs and blankets."

"I-I don't know, Keith, it sounds kind of risky. What if someone sees us sneaking into the trucks?"

"Yeah, Jacc's right. It's called trespassing. They could call the police." Keith nodded. "I know there are risks, but what choice do we have? We can find another shelter, ride the trains, or blow our money on a flee-bag hotel." I ran my fingers through my hair and let out a long sigh. Keith was right. There weren't many options. Sleeping in a U-Haul truck was risky, but it would keep us out of the elements and we might get a decent night's sleep.

"Okay, so, where the heck do we find a fleet of trucks?"

"Jacc, that's not a problem. There's a lot not far from here."

"I sure hope you two know what you're doing. I don't feel comfortable with this plan at all. It just sounds too risky."

"Now that that's settled," Keith said, "let's go grab a shower." As we headed back to the train, I prayed Diane's fears wouldn't come back to haunt us.

DOWN THROUGH THE YEARS

Reflections Of My Life

Down through the years, I've rejoiced with my peers
And celebrated with cheers
Down through the years, I shed a lot of tears
And faced a lot of fears
Down through the years, I've had to shift gears
And change careers
Down through the years, I've endured jealous sneers
And rumor smears
Down through the years, I've been a pioneer
And even dwelled in a frontier
Down through the years, I've lost in love
And gained wisdom from above
Finally understanding all that
Has happened down through the years

–Jacc –

Chapter Five

THE CHICAGO Park District offered free showers at several local field houses. The one downtown produced the hottest water. The only drawback was we weren't allowed to store our belongings in any of the field house lockers. The staff was constantly tossing someone's belongings in the garbage when they discovered their stash.

Once we arrived, we signed in at the front desk. I could see Diane was especially glad to discover there wasn't anyone ahead of us on the list. The relief on her face when she found out she would have the women's shower all to herself was apparent. It was obvious she was still feeling embarrassed about her hair. I knew it would take some time for her to emotionally heal. "Diane, we'll meet you at the front desk when we're done."

"All right, Jacc, I'll see you guys later."

Every muscle in my body relaxed as the hot water washed away yesterday's grime. I stood in the shower and let the water cleanse me physically as well as mentally. There's definitely something about water that purifies the soul. No wonder it's used so often in religious rites. It's amazing how one can take for granted the simple things in life such as a shower, a bathtub, and even a clothes closet. For the homeless these things were a luxury.

Never in my life was I so glad to just be able to bathe. The only thing I looked forward to every night at the D'Row was being able to take a shower. Before I became homeless, it never occurred to me how blessed I was to have a bathroom and a closet. Prior to my plight, I was clueless as to what it really meant to be without.

Although being homeless was a humbling experience, it also became a fuel of strength for me. It made me reevaluate my life and my priorities. I, like so many others, used to feel I was entitled to life's luxuries just because I happened to be born both in the "right" country and of the "right" skin color. I was also conditioned to think that if I just went with the flow and dotted all my *I*'s and crossed all my *T*'s, I'd always come out on top. Homelessness had taught me different. It taught me that no matter how hard you try in life, the measure of your success would always be codependent on two factors. The first and far most important is all blessings are a true gift from God. If I've achieved any measure of success in my life it's because he had made it all possible. The second factor is God doesn't act alone. He strategically uses people to open doors for you. There are people who are strategically placed in your life to be a blessing just like there are people who are strategically in your life to be a hindrance. He does this through man's own free will and the softening of his heart. I've often wondered why there's so much suffering in the world? There's something about being stripped of all your worldly possessions that brings you closer to God. Now that I've actually experienced what it is to have lost everything, I realize they weren't what really mattered. What really mattered is that I had my health, a strong mental mind, and a pure heart. Those of us who are on this "trail of life" are considered the lower form of humanity, yet we are as royal ambassadors to God. We are small and minute, yet we stand tall. We have few tools, yet we're resourceful and wise. We dwell on all five continents of the earth from Africa, to the Americas, to Asia, Australia, and Europe.

We're male and female, both young and old. We're husbands, wives, sisters, brothers, cousins, aunts, uncles, mothers, fathers, daughters, sons, grandparents, and even children. We're Christians, Muslims, Buddhists, Hindus, Jews, Spiritualists, and some are atheists. We're friends, lovers, associates, neighbors, strangers, and yes, even sometimes enemies. We're from all types of backgrounds, professional, unprofessional, educated, uneducated, skilled and unskilled. We're the inhabitants of the world. We are the homeless.

As I stepped out of the shower and dried off, I finally understood why I'd personally been chosen to walk down this path. I knew that God had a calling and a greater purpose for me, but in order for me to be able to fulfill my destiny, I had to be in a position of not only humbleness and compassion, I also needed to learn to lean completely on him and be willing to do his bidding.

Yes, God had a divine plan for me, and as sure as my name is Jaccson Ford, I knew Diane was a major part of it. There was definitely a reason why our paths had crossed, why he'd allowed us to meet. She was truly a rose in the dessert. Her inner strength outweighed any of her adversaries' fiery darts. It was an inner strength that could not be denied, and at best, could only be admired. Quickly getting dress, I wondered how she was fairing. Keith had already showered, shaved, and gotten dressed. Glad I hadn't cut myself while shaving; I rinsed my face, brushed my teeth, and finally headed out the door.

The line was just dying down by the time we arrived at a nearby soup kitchen for dinner. Since I'd never been to that particular soup kitchen, I was surprised to see it was located in the heart of downtown, off of Michigan Ave. From what Keith and Diane had told me, the meals weren't much and there were no seconds so most people usually walked down to lower Wacker Drive afterwards to wait for another church to deliver their famous soul food.

I can attest Keith and Diane hadn't exaggerated. Tonight's meal consisted of a salad, a half a spoonful of green beans, and a small slice of ham. The dessert was one cookie and there was only water to drink. What I found troubling about the place was as we were leaving after dinner, I noticed the volunteers were busy stuffing their faces with all the leftover food from the meal. This struck me as kind of strange because the soup kitchen coordinator had poignantly let everyone know there wouldn't be any seconds during her speech just before dinner was served. She also turned away several latecomers, explaining that there wasn't any more food left. It was only as we were walking in a single file line pass the kitchen, that I witnessed the volunteers along with the coordinator feasting on the leftovers. No wonder they quickly gathered up all the food and hurried into the kitchen right after the last person in line was served during dinner.

Needless to say, Diane, Keith, and I followed the crowd to Lower Wacker Drive. By the time we arrived, a line had already formed. People were standing around waiting for a church van to pull up. I'd heard that a large population of homeless people slept under the cold and filthy drive, but I was surprised to see so many women with small children standing near their sleeping gear. One of the women walked up to Diane. "Can I buy a cigarette off you?"

"Sorry, I don't smoke." She turned to me. "What about you?" I shook my head. "Sorry." Keith threw up his hands and shook his head as well. "Damn. I'm feenin for a smoke. Times are hard on the boulevard. This is when we need the moneyman to show up." My brows lifted. "The moneyman, who's he?" Keith turned to me. "I've heard about him. Supposedly he comes down here every year, usually around Christmas and passes out hundred dollar bills. No one really knows who he is, except he's some rich white guy who's been coming down here for years. One year some stud snatched his moneybag and ran. Folks thought he wasn't going to show up anymore after that, but he surprised everyone and came back the next year. I guess he didn't want to disappoint the people. Anyway, he's been bringing bodyguards ever since that incident, and there hasn't been any more trouble."

"That's right," the woman confirmed. "Hey, Moe! Let me get one of those squares up out ya!" She suddenly ran after a man she'd spotted with a cigarette dangling from his mouth. Just then people started to tighten up the line as a white van slowly drove up and stopped. Several doors opened as people piled out and walked around to the back of the van. They started unloading the food and supplies they'd brought.

"All right! A male volunteer yelled. "Women and children are served first. Gentlemen, let the ladies come up to the front of line!" Women started walking toward the front and Keith nudged Diane to follow suit. A little unsure, she followed the crowd of women. The meal was an ample helping of cabbage, corn-beef, cornbread, sweet potatoes, and fruit juice. The line moved quickly and it wasn't long before Diane, Keith, and I received our food. Deciding the lower drive was too dirty for us to enjoy it; we carried our Styrofoam containers out onto the main street and headed to a park to eat. Finally reaching the park, we found a bench and sat down. Too hungry to engage in any conversation, we eat our food in silence.

The images of the women and children we'd left behind still lingered in my mind as I finished off my food. The very thought of those children huddled in that cold and dirty underground as their mothers fended off rats and heaven knows what else was heart-wrenching to say the least. A sudden urgency swept over me as I thought about the alleged moneyman who'd been coming around for years. He definitely had the right idea. It was obvious he was doing it from his heart and not for notoriety since he'd managed to keep his name and identity a secret.

I've always felt many were more than happy to jump on what I term "The feel good" bandwagon. They often did a charitable deed so they could pat themselves on the back and feel good about the accolades they receive. I commended the moneyman for taking the initiative and making a personal contribution that went directly to the people without all the fanfare and hoopla. Giving back to mankind should definitely come from the heart, and be done without praise, hidden agendas, and systematic control through social programs. It's just the decent and humane thing to do, especially when you see that the need of the people are great, and it's in the power of your hand to be a blessing. Somehow I felt the moneyman had listened to his conscious and hearkened to his calling just as I knew I'd eventually do. The more I thought about it, the more I realized the time was coming when my calling would become crystal clear. The urgency I kept feeling deep within my soul was a testament to it. The rain started coming down just as we began packing up to leave. Glad that we at least had a dry place to sleep tonight, we ran to catch the trolley.

"All right, everybody, it's time to go! N-nowww!" A thunderous male voice could be heard throughout the lot as the back doors of the U-haul trucks were raised. The angry voice woke us up as we lay snuggled nice and warm inside of one of the trucks. Keith had successfully led us to the fleet of trucks, and to our surprise, there were lots of wool blankets inside. We'd managed to get in several hours of sleep up until now. A loud thumping sound could be heard banging against the outside of the trucks as the man repeatedly chased the occupants out. Not sure what to do, we were momentarily paralyzed with fear. "J-Jacc, what are we going to do?" Diane whispered.

"I-I don't know. Maybe if we're real quiet, he'll pass this truck up."

"I think it's too late for that," Keith said when the back door of the truck was suddenly raised and a stocky man with a baseball bat stood looking at us. "Well, well, look what we have here. Three little pigs wrapped in blankets. I want you out of here, now!"

"All right, all right, we're getting up. Just take it easy."

Keith got up and grabbed his jacket as I helped Diane up. Haphazardly putting on our coats, we grabbed our belongings and climbed out of the truck. "And don't come back!" the man yelled as we began walking away.

"I'm sick and tired of you homeless bums hanging around this here yard. Next time I catch you round here, I'm calling the cops!"

We walked to the next block before Diane stopped.

"Is there any place we can go without being run off?" Keith looked at us. "Well, I don't know about you two, but I've had it up to here with Chicago. I was going to tell you guys in the morning, but I might as well let you know now."

"*Let us know what?*" our voice rang out. "I'm heading to Indiana. There's a lot of wooded area up there, places where a person can dwell and no one will bother you. Besides, it's cheaper to live in Indiana."

Diane and I glanced at each other. I wasn't sure if I bought into the whole "we'll fair better off in Indiana" premise, however, I was open to leaving town if she was.

"What do you think?" Her weary eyes held mine as she shrugged. "I guess it couldn't hurt. I'm just so tired of moving around." Touching her cheek, I sighed. "I know, but at least we have each other." She nodded and turned to Keith. "I guess we're going with you."

"Good. We might as well head down to the rail station. The first train for Indiana leaves around 6:00 a.m.

Five hours later, we found ourselves trekking through a forest preserve near Wolf Lake, which borders Hammond, Indiana, and Chicago. Once we arrived in Hammond, Diane and I stopped off at a local grocery store and brought a fair amount of nonperishable food while Keith visited a local thrift store to pick up several blankets. Afterwards, we met up and began our long hike through the wooded area. It seemed like we'd been walking for hours and frankly I wasn't sure how long Diane could hold out. She looked like she was ready to stop right in her tracks and set up camp.

"Hey, Keith, how much further, I don't think we can take anymore forging through these woods?"

"Yeah," Diane added. "I'm beat. Can't we just stop here?" Keith stopped and placed his backpack down.

"Actually this is exactly where I was going to suggest we camp." Glad we'd finally stopped; Diane dropped her backpack and flopped down in the grass with a sigh of relief.

"Thank God," she said as she stretched her legs out in front of her and leaned back on her arms for support.

"This is as good a place to camp as any." Keith tossed her a blanket as he began unpacking the sleeping gear. I started unloading the food. Holding up two cans, I waited for their vote. "Which one? We've got beans or ravioli to go with the franks."

"*The beans*," they said. "Yeah, I guess you're right. They do taste better with hotdogs."

Putting away the can of ravioli, I gathered up some wood and started a fire.

Once the fire was in full commission, Diane took over preparing the meal while Keith and I sat round and chatted. After our recent ordeal, we just wanted to forget about our troubles and relax. As down and out, and as homeless as we were, being out in the woods like this somehow made us feel free and liberated. That night sitting around chewing the fat with Keith and Diane turned out to be one of the best nights I'd had in a long time. Everything was perfect, the meal, the company, and the stars were shinning so bright, I could have sworn one of them winked at me. We talked into the wee hours of the mornings, finally drifting off to sleep around 2:00 a.m.

"Peeaannutt! Peanut! Come, here boy!"

"W-what the hell?" I woke up to a not so friendly dog tugging on my blanket with his teeth. Rolling over, I barely managed to escape his fangs.

"Hey!" Diane yelled as she also jumped up. Quickly picking up a large stick, she prepared herself to do battle with the mutt.

"Don't you dare hit my dog!" A young blond boy with the bluest eyes I'd ever seen suddenly ran up to her and knocked the stick out of her hand. He was a scrawny little tike, couldn't have been no older than eleven, yet he looked like he was ready to take on the world for the love of his dog. Quickly scrambling to my feet, I approached the boy.

"Look, we don't want any trouble. Just call off your dog and we'll pack up peacefully."

"Aww, mister, you ain't gotta leave on account of me and my dog. This ain't our turf or anything. We were just chasing rabbits. Our camp is up yonder. We best be getting back. They'll be looking for us if we're gone too long. Come on, boy, let's go." Slapping his hands on his knees, the lad called his dog. Complying, the dog ran to him and excitedly wagged his tail. "Hey, Jacc!" Keith hollered as he walked toward us.

"There's some people camping further down by the lake!"

"Yep," the young boy nodded. "That'll be my camp."

"Hello," Keith said once he reached us. "I see we have a visitor. What's your name son?"

"My name's Raymond, but you can call me Bones. Everybody does on account they say I'm more bones than skin."

We burst out laughing. Raymond or "Bones" as he suggested we call him was quite a character. "Alright, Bones, nice to meet you." Keith shook the lad's hand. "You know anything about the folks camping down there by the lake?"

"Sure do. That'll be my ma, my sister and brothers, Daryl, Hattie, and old Papa Joe. We've been sleeping in these woods for about a year. Everyone's real nice. Daryl acts tough, but deep down, he's a good guy. He's been looking out for us on account they say my ma's a little touched in the head. It happened a few years back, but she's slowly getting better. We met Hattie and Papa Joe when we came to the woods. Hattie says the woods have a way of healing the soul. Say why don't ya'll come and have breakfast with us. Hattie makes the best flapjacks and there's always plenty. She won't mind, honestly. She's always rounding up some grub for folks passing through."

Diane smiled. "You know, Bones, for a little guy, you sure have a lot to say. Sorry about your dog. I didn't mean to scare you."

"Aww, shucks, lady, you didn't scare me or old Peanut. I was more worried about him tearing into you than you hurting him. Hitting him with that stick would have made him sure enough mad. He's a good hunting dog. I've had him for a while. Daryl gave him to me when he was just a pup. Say, you coming or not? I gotta get going before Daryl skins me alive!"

"Sure," Diane said between chuckles. "We'd be more than pleased to join you for breakfast. My name is Diane. This is Jacc and Keith. I hope we can all be friends." She stuck out her hand and Bone's slapped her five. Glad to see that we'd made our peace with Bones and his dog, I quickly gathered up our bedding while Keith and Diane gathered up the food. As soon as everything was packed, I turned to Bones. "All right, young man, lead the way. We'd better hurry. We don't want them skinning what little skin you have left on your bones!" Our laughter rang out as we followed behind Bones and his trusty companion, Peanut.

"Bones! Boy, where the hell have you been?" A stocky black man with long cornrows, a mustache, and goatee swatted Bones over the head as we stood in the middle of the campground. Several picnic tables and barbeque grills were scattered throughout the grounds, and in the not too far distance, stood an older white woman under a canopied gazebo. The smell of bacon, pancakes, hot maple syrup, and to my delight, cheese-eggs filled the air. "Aww, Darryl, Peanut and me were chasing rabbits."

"Boy, didn't I tell you to leave those damn rabbits alone? You can get rabies from wild animals. Why you gotta be so hardheaded? Go on, and get washed up. Hattie's bout ready to put the breakfast on the table." He swatted Bones one more time as the child ran off.

"How ya'll doing? Name's Daryl. I take it Bones invited you folks to breakfast?"

"Uh, yeah, we hope it's alright. We don't want to put a strain on you if you don't have enough food. I'm Jacc. This is Diane and Keith."

"Man, are you kidding? There's plenty. Come on." We followed Daryl as he started walking toward a picnic table. "Hey, Hattie, we got three joining us!" The older woman wiped her hands on her smock and stepped out from inside the gazebo. "I got eyes. I can see that. Morning, folks, you welcome to join us. There's more than enough. Only thing I ask is make sure you eat everything on your plate. There's just too many starving folks in the world to waste food." Hattie handed Diane some plates. "Here, darlin, you mind setting the table?"

"No, not at all."

"Glad to hear it. I don't know where Clarice has gotten to. She usually helps me set the table. Bones go see if your ma is down by the lake with the rest of the youngins."

"That won't be necessary," an older black man said as he walked up with a thin blond white woman and three small children trailing behind him. "Morning, folks, guess everyone's here. What ya'll standing round for? Sit so Hattie can bless the food and we can eat." Following his cue, we sat down as Hattie placed the last items on the table in preparation for the meal. Finally sitting herself, she looked around at everyone. "Before I say grace, I think it's only befitting for everyone to introduce themselves. I like to know who I'm breaking bread with. Let me start off. I'm Hattie May, and this here is Papa Joe, my old man. Ya'll know Bones, scrawny little thing for twelve ain't he? Clarice is his ma, and then you have Amanda, his sister, she's five.

Then there's Bone's brothers, Thomas and James, their eight and nine."

Daryl's brows turned up in a frown. "Damn, I guess I don't count."

Hattie's eyes shot daggers at him. His tough guy persona didn't intimidate her in the least. "Pipe down. I was getting to you." Her eyes quickly zeroed in on me. "This here is Daryl, as you'll soon find out, his bark is much worse than his bite. And who might you be?"

I could feel all eyes on me as everyone waited for me to speak. I looked at Hattie. "My name's Jaccson, but everyone calls me Jacc."

"It's a pleasure to meet you, Jacc. I reckon you're nice and hungry?" Smiling, I nodded. "Yes, ma'am, I am. It's very kind of you to share your food with me and my friends."

"It's no problem whatsoever. If your friends don't mind introducing themselves, I'll bless the food then we can eat." Taking the hint, Diane smiled at Hattie. "Hi, I'm Diane. I'd also like to thank you for being so kind."

"That's right," Keith added. "I'm Keith, and, ma'am, if you don't mind, I'd like to say the blessing this morning." Hattie's face lit up in a smile. Very spiritually minded, she was more than glad to have another praying person at the table. "Young man, you're definitely a fella after my heart. By all means, go ahead and bless the food!" Bowing our heads, we paid homage to the good Lord as Keith blessed the food. Hands began reaching for the containers of food the moment our voices rang out in Amen. "Pass the salt," Daryl said as he scooped up a heap of eggs and handed the bowl to me. Piling some eggs on my plate, I passed the bowl as Papa Joe handed Daryl the salt. "Tell me, Jacc," the old man said in between chewing his food, "where about do you folks come from?"

"We're from Chicago, but things weren't working out for us there so we decided we'd try our hand in Indiana." Nodding, Papa Joe took a sip of orange juice.

"Yeah, I know what you mean. We've been dwelling around these here parts for some years now. Don't think I'll ever return to Chi-town. It's a mean city. We used to sleep under the back stairway of a church while we were there. It was a good spot, except when it rained, the damn thing leaked something awful."

"Yeah, all our blankets would get wet," Hattie added.

"Never did like those damn shelters. I've always encountered problems while staying in them. I think it's why a lot of homeless folks absolutely refuse to stay in the shelter. Problem is poor folks are treated like a social disease. Seems like the only solution them damn social agencies can give to the poor man is to provide shelters that are run no better than a prison. I'd just like to know when did being poor become a sin or a crime? And who the hell started calling it a social disease? Them damn caseworkers that run them places don't have a clue about being homeless. Sure they have the book smarts, but they don't know how to really fix the problem.

They think they can case-manage another human being's life. Hell, there isn't a blueprint to living life. You just live it by experiencing the ups and downs of it all."

I noticed a sudden sadness washed over Diane as she listened to Hattie. It was obvious she was reliving her recent traumatic experience. Hattie noticed Diane's change in mood as well. "What's the matter, honey? Was it something I said that's put that long look on your face?" Realizing that she was revealing more than she'd intended Diane instantly changed her expression as a mask came up, cloaking her true feelings like a closely woven veil. Offering a smile, she said, "Oh, no, please don't think you've said anything wrong. Trust me, Hattie, it isn't you at all. It's just sad that so many have put their trust in the shelter system. They think that they're going to be a safe haven for them then they find out they're actually victimization dens."

"Hmmm," Hattie said, "from the way you talk, girlie, I'd say you have your own war stories to tell." Not sure what to say, Diane glanced at me. "Why don't we toast to better days and not dwell on life's sadness?" Keith raised his cup and waited for everyone to follow suit as he threw me a sly grin. It was obvious we were on the same wavelength. We both wanted to spare Diane the aggravation of having to divulge personal information she wasn't ready to share. "I agree. Let's focus on what's ahead of us and the future."

Everyone raised their cups and drank to a future we

all hoped someday would be bright and stable even though it looked uncertain at the moment.

"Jacc, do you like poetry?" The question came as a complete surprise to me, a pleasant one, yet a surprise all the same. I was very much into poetry and I often wrote long expressive ones in my leisure. Diane and I were stretched out on a blanket staring up at the beautiful clear sky the next day. I turned on my side and looked at her. She was still wearing Keith's baseball cap. It certainly came in handy for blocking out the sun's strong rays. "Yes, Diane, I do. As a matter of fact, I love to write poetry." Surprised by my answer, she sat up and stared at me. "You're kidding?"

"No, it's true. I'm a poet at heart."

"Wow, that's truly a coincidence. I'm also a poet at heart. Poetry is in my soul. I began writing as a girl when I felt like there was no one to listen to my troubles, so I'd just right to God. Somehow I knew I could always tell him my problems. I'd pretend I was writing him a letter and the words just began to flow. Now any time I feel like life is getting to be too much to handle, I just find a quiet place and jump into my creative zone. Writing can be very therapeutic." Reaching up, I touched the side of her face.

"You're right. Writing allows a person to venture deep within their mind where true healing begins. I knew there was a reason why we connect the way we do. We're both expressive people who are also independent thinkers."

She smiled reflectively. "Yes, we are. I don't know why I was surprised to learn you wrote poetry. It makes perfect sense that you'd enjoy writing. You're a very insightful and compassionate person who cares about what matters most. Say, why don't we spend the rest of the afternoon doing what we both love?"

She reached for her backpack and took out two notebooks and a couple of pens." Accepting a notebook from her, I smiled. "Sure, why not? I haven't written anything in a while although I've been putting some things together in my head." Settling down, we both jumped into our zone and wrote for hours in silence before we finally decided to share what we'd written with each other. Very impressed with one another's work, we decided to collaborate on a poem together. It was well into the evening before we finally packed up our belongings and headed back to camp. Another glorious day spent together with Diane was the last thing I thought about later that night as I drifted off to sleep.

LOVE THY SELF

Nurturing One's Own Soul

When no one loved me, I learned to love myself
When no one believes in you, believe in yourself
To every man, woman, boy, girl, love thyself!
When no one will extend them self
Help yourself
You may have to walk alone
But don't despair, because all hope isn't gone
Remember, there's One that sticks closer than a
brother
He'll protect you like no other
He steps in when all run away
He'll carry you all the way
He becomes your best promoter, rooting and cheering
you on
Even when you feel victory is forgone
So, I say, love thyself!
Promote oneself!
Believe in yourself!
As I believe in me
Then you'll see
How much wiser you'll be

–Diane –

*C*hapter Six

ALTHOUGH it's been several weeks since we first left the shelter, I was still amazed how well we were surviving outdoors. I thought about how the early American settlers must have felt living a nomadic lifestyle. If they could survive the harsh elements of outdoors, why is it people in today's world find it so reproachable? Before the world was as modernized as it is now, people lived without the technology that's available today. Yet, through it all, man has survived. My generation, the generation before me, and the generation that's coming after me, was, is, and will continue to be a testament of man's survival.

These thoughts raced through my mind as I sat by the lake with Diane. For the past few days I'd been feeling more anxious than usual. An idea that I'd been tossing around in my mind for a while has nagged at me for the past few days. As I watched Diane toss some bread to a flock of hungry ducks, I decided to put my idea to her.

"I've been thinking about this for a while. I want to build houses for the homeless. You said it yourself; the real root to homelessness is poverty. If you think about it, paying rent every month doesn't help the situation."

Tossing out the last bit of bread, she turned to me and gave me one of her usual looks when she thought I'd said something completely crazy. "You think being responsible for a mortgage is the solution? Come on, Jacc, that doesn't make sense."

"Who said anything about paying a mortgage? In my book paying a mortgage is just as bad as paying rent. It takes the average person about thirty years or more to finally pay off their home. Mortgages are just as big of a trap as renting. Do you know how many people are losing their homes because they can't make their mortgage payments? The turnover rate for the middle class losing their homes through foreclosure is almost as high as it is for a renter who's been evicted from their apartment. Hell, middle class America is struggling to keep a roof over their own head! No, mortgages aren't the answer. What I want to do is build houses specifically for the homeless at an affordable price. My plan is to set an affordable price ceiling for all the homes that are built. It wouldn't matter about the size and cost to build the homes. I wouldn't spare any expense in making sure these were beautiful homes."

"So what you're saying is all the houses would cost the same, regardless of design and size?"

"That's right. It makes perfect sense to be a homeowner verses paying rent. The benefits are far more beneficial. For starters, you have complete control of your property as a homeowner. Owning your home allows you to build equity. If you think about it, a renter pays for the privilege of living in an apartment with no potential of actually owning it. Besides saving money on your federal taxes, there's also a sense of pride in owning your own home. The problem with the system today is it takes too long for a person to finally pay off their home. That's because the Average home is just like everything else in this country, overpriced. What choice does a person have than to take out a thirty year mortgage? The realtors, developers, and the finance companies are getting rich while Americans are struggling to own a piece of the American dream. We can't win for losing."

"Okay, I see your point, but honestly, Jacc, purchasing a home is a major step and there's already a stigma associated with homeless people being lazy, uneducated, and lack the skills to manage money. Who'd back such an idea let alone finance it? After all, it takes major dollars to pull off what you're suggesting. Heck, the US government isn't even willing to sacrifice the kind of money that's really needed."

I nodded. "You're right. The government doesn't want to directly provide money to build actual homes for the homeless. They'd rather give billions in grant money to programs like HUD and Section 8 who in turn allocate so much of the money to shelters and social agencies that are more interested in trying to cure addictions and medicate the mentally ill instead of addressing America's rapidly growing housing crisis. As long as the government blatantly chooses to ignore the truth about what causes homelessness and allow social agencies to mask the problem behind unrealistic social reforms, there'll never be a solution to the problem."

"Jacc, if you're waiting on the government to

suddenly grow a serious social and moral conscious, forget it. Why fantasize about homelessness being a thing of the past when we can't even count on our government to help with the problem? Face it, the situation is hopeless."

"I wouldn't say it's completely hopeless. Besides, faith is what's needed to bring about change. Without it, Diane, all will truly be lost. I don't necessarily live with the hope that this country's political leaders will step up to the plate. No, I feel there's going to come a time when the poor will have an opportunity to truly live above the substandard conditions they currently face today. I do believe God is going to call forth someone to create a successful way for the poor to be able to finally afford their own homes."

"Even if such a person existed, Jacc, how is setting a price ceiling going to help the homeless pay for the homes? Sure, your idea may help the middle class who already have somewhat of a decent income to work with not to mention possible savings. Even if the home is priced way below market value, the homeless certainly don't have a viable way to save the money for an outright purchase."

"I've thought long and hard about a successful way for them to purchase their homes. All they really need is enough time allotted for them to save the money. As we both know most of the homeless aren't completely without financial resources or income. Many of them get a monthly check either through SSI, or they're able to hold down some type of low paying job. What I propose is instead of the homeless being warehoused in what we know as traditional shelters, they should be allowed to live for a couple of years rent-free in an actual apartment and save their money. After the two-year grace period, they outright purchase a home provided by an organization that's not for capital gain, but was formed for the sole purpose of providing affordable homes exclusively for the homeless. They would also provide the temporary apartments for them until they were actually able to purchase the homes." I could see Diane was impressed with my idea, although I knew she didn't totally buy it.

"Wow," she said, "looks like you've given this some serious thought. If only something like that were really possible. It sounds feasible, in fact it's a brilliant plan, but it takes major dollars to pull off something like that. I doubt there is an organization let alone a soul on this earth who'd be willing to extend them self and step outside of the box to really offer that kind of financial help to the poor. I used to also dream about fixing the problem of homelessness. I'd often say if I were rich, I'd bless the homeless with real homes to live in, but like I said it was just a fantasy. I doubt seriously if we'll ever see homelessness disappear."

"Diane, I know it's hard to believe the situation can change, but it's possible. As it stands the homeless population is growing by leaps and bounds. It's getting harder to classify exactly who is considered homeless. One minute you read those living in shelters and don't have a fixed or steady address is homeless, then the next minute you read those living with family and friends are homeless. Then you have a whole population of homeless children who often are part of the foster care system. Children living in foster homes are also considered homeless. They grow up developing a nomadic syndrome. Former foster children often end up actually living on the streets just as military veterans do."

"Don't forget about the hidden homeless," she added. "It's really hard to detect them since they aren't dirty or smelly and actually have full time jobs yet can't afford housing. Look at us, we don't fit the classic textbook image of a homeless person, yet we are."

I nodded. "You're right, we don't fit the image of the Bowery Bum. There are more of us out here than society is ready or willing to admit. Sooner or later the issue of what's really causing the problem has to be addressed. As more educated and middle class people experience layoffs, foreclosures, and even health issues that eventually classify them as disable, they'll start to realize we're all living behind a thin veil known as a safety net. As much as society wants to turn and look the other way, the time is coming when this growing problem won't be able to be ignored. Most Americans are way over their heads in debt with credit cards payments, mortgages, car payments, student loans, and hospital bills. You can't turn on the TV without some talk show showing a segment about money management and savings."

"What savings?" Diane asked cynically. "The poor don't make enough to save. Most are literally living paycheck to paycheck. The middle class aren't fairing any better although they like to think they are by keeping up with the Joneses. Sure, they might have some savings tied into CDs, or a 401k, but many of them end up dipping into their savings when unexpected financial crises occur. As far as the rich is concerned, they're too worried about maintaining the wealth they've managed to acquire. They know it's not enough to make millions, but the key for them is to maintain it. Jacc, your plan is definitely insightful and probably plausible, but realistically, I don't think it'll ever come to fruition. I just don't see it happening because the bottom line is no one gives a damn about the homeless. Most are too busy trying to uphold their own status quo. There isn't going to be an organization or a Robin Hood who'll liberate the poor. If ever there is, I'll be the first to offer my assistance. You're as much of a dreamer as I am, but realistically we can't live in a dream world because homelessness is a very real situation for millions of people. As much as we'd like to see the poor be blessed to that magnitude, there just aren't enough real selfless and compassionate people in the world."

Glad she liked my plan, I knew given the chance, Diane would also be just as giving of herself as I would.

Realizing we'd spent the last hour debating something that wasn't going to be solved overnight; I decided to change the subject. It took a long systematic process for Americans to wind up living on the streets and it was going to take a long process to get people off of them.

"I got one! Wow! Look, Jacc, I actually caught one!"

"You sure did, Bones. That's terrific!" Several days later, all the men along with Bones and his brothers were hanging out at the lake. We'd gotten up at the crack of dawn with the hope of having an early start on some serious fishing. Hattie was counting on us to catch enough to feed a small army. She was planning on having a fish fry later that evening in celebration of Papa's Joe's 65th birthday. Originally from Mississippi, all he talked about lately was the fish fries his family had every Friday when he was a little boy. According to Papa Joe, the best time to go fishing was right around sunrise. I think the fish must have been aware of this strategy because we'd been at it for nearly five hours and the most any of us have been able to get was a nibble here and there. It was now mid-morning.

"Hey, Bones! That's awesome, man! It's about time somebody caught something." Daryl jumped up and rushed over to him as he struggled to hold on to the fish. "Hot damn!" Papa Joe said as he also offered his assistance.

"Steady there, boy. Don't let her get away. She's a big one!" Bone's face was full of pride when he finally managed to reel the fish in. He held it up for several minutes while Daryl snapped some pictures from a Polaroid camera.

I was happy for Bones. He needed to feel a sense of accomplishment. Being homeless was hard enough for adults, but for a boy his age it was especially hard. Besides his little brothers, there were no other children his age around to play with. He'd told me the children that attended his school often teased him and his siblings because they were homeless. I suddenly thought about a conversation I'd had with Daryl a couple of days ago.

According to Daryl, he first met Clarice and her children while living in a shelter in Chicago. The shelter administrators didn't really know what to do about the situation since they didn't take in families with children. While they were trying to hammer out a solution, Clarice was struggling to fight off the constant harassment from both the homeless men and women in the shelter. The other women were jealous that the men were befriending her. Never mind the fact they were only doing it because they were secretly plotting to turn Clarice into the next crack whore.

A small, quite woman, Clarice tried to keep to herself as much as possible until one day she followed one of the men to a place he claimed she could take a shower. The shelter had restricted the residents to only showering twice a week. Desperately wanting a shower, she went with him only to find herself held up in a crack house with several of the guys from the shelter. They brutally gang raped her as she unsuccessfully fought them off. The ordeal left her emotionally traumatized and scared. She completely shut down and stopped talking all together. Listening to Daryl explain Clarice's horrific ordeal helped me understand why even to this day she still didn't speak. It certainly shed some insight into why she's considered to be touched in the head.

Daryl went on to explain rumors started flying as word on the street got out about what had happened to Clarice. Things came to blows one evening at dinner when he could no longer endure the talk that was swirling all around him. Several guys were bragging about their evil deed, even claiming they were going to go back for a second round. Flipping out, Daryl stood up and yelled for them to shut up. Shouting it wasn't any of his business, one of the guys stood up as well. Soon a fight broke out which caused Daryl to be thrown out of the shelter leaving Clarice behind.

No sooner, however, had Daryl been thrown out, the shelter arranged for Clarice and her children to be transported to another shelter that was supposedly more equipped to handle homeless women and children. Only it really wasn't. From the moment Clarice entered the shelter, she was assigned a case manager who began pushing very hard to have her admitted to a living facility for the mentally ill. The shelter also had a nurse on staff that worked closely with a psychiatrist who often held weekly mental health meetings at the shelter in hopes of getting the residents to agree to get treatment. The ultimate plan was to have Clarice live in a supervised mentally ill nursing home while the children were placed in foster care.

Daryl got wind of what was going on when Bones came looking for him one day and begged him to help his family leave the shelter. The boy was in tears as he pleaded for help. He said the shelter had Clarice on all type of medication. She'd sometimes walk around looking lethargic or she'd just sit around like a zombie, staring off into space. Agreeing to help them, Daryl snuck Clarice and the children out of the shelter later that night. From there they headed to Indiana. They settled into another shelter and enrolled the children in school. However, their stay in that shelter was short lived because the shelter said they didn't house couples or entire families. That's when they made their way to the woods.

They never told the school officials the children were no longer living in the shelter. Daryl didn't want to take the risk of the children being taken from Clarice. He'd fought real hard to keep the entire family together. Although they weren't his biological kids, he loved them as if they were. I learned so much about Daryl's personality that day as we stood by the lake and talked. To the world he appeared to be the average street thug who hadn't amounted to much, but to me, he was what epitomized the true character of a man. Fearlessly protective of those he loved, he'd gone against the grain to make sure they were safe. Daryl may not realize he was making a difference in this world, but it was obvious in the way Clarice's eyes lit every time she saw him. It was also obvious the way he and Bone's seem to have a natural bond.

That bond was very visible right now as I watched Daryl playfully ruffle Bone's hair before slapping him high five. It made me feel good to know Bones had a male role model that accepted him for who he was and didn't put added pressure on him the way my father use to do to me.

After Bone's big catch, we all finally started having some luck of our own. By the time we were done and ready to head back to camp, we had two buckets full of fish.

The women were busy setting up everything for the fish fry when we finally reached the camp. Earlier, Hattie had managed to convince Diane to tag along with them into Hammond. Hattie needed to stock up on some supplies for this evening's gala event. She'd also mentioned something about stopping off at a little shop where the women could buy something special for themselves. It was a little ritual they did whenever they went into town to shop. I'd noticed she and Diane had grown close over the past weeks. I'd often see them sitting off by themselves. At times it looked like they were engaged in a serious conversation. I was glad Hattie had managed to convince Diane to go with them on their outing.

I hoped she'd had a good time and had bought something really special for herself. I didn't have to wait long to find out.

I immediately spotted her the moment we reached the camp. I couldn't believe my eyes. Diane nervously took two steps before she stopped. I was absolutely speechless. She looked just as beautiful as the first day I'd seen her. Stunned, I could only stare. "J-Jacc, do you l-like it? Oh, God, you hate it! Hattie, I told you this was a bad idea. I look foolish wearing this thing!" She suddenly turned and ran. "Diane! Wait! Come back! Damn, what an idiot! I was staring at her like a dumfounded schoolboy. Damn, damn, damn!"

"Wow, was that Diane? Keith turned to me.

"Yeah," I said still feeling stunned. "What happened?" Keith pressed further. "Why'd she run off like that?"

"I don't know."

"I'll tell you what happened," Daryl said as he set a bucket of fish down, "The woman wanted you to tell her she looked good, instead of you just stood there. You should have told her how fine she looked, but you were acting like you'd just swallowed your tongue."

"You're right. I guess I was taken by surprise. She looks, it looks so natural."

"You damn right it does," Hattie added. "I helped her pick it out. She told me what those bastards at that shelter did to her hair. They tried to destroy her, but they didn't succeed. Something similar happened to a friend of mine that stayed at one of them awful places. Only it just didn't happen to her. There were about a dozen women who woke up one morning and discovered they were either completely bald or they had large bald patches in their scalp. Now you tell me, how the hell does something like that happen? You just don't go to bed one night and the next morning you don't have any hair! I thought it would be a good idea for Diane to buy a wig. I figured it would lift her spirits and give her back her confidence. She wouldn't have to keep hiding behind that damn baseball cap. She could feel pretty, like a woman again. We shopped around until we found one that fits her face. Its real human hair and she looks damn good in it."

Feeling like a complete jerk, I nodded. "Yes, she does, Hattie. She's beautiful."

"Don't tell me. I suggest you go after her and tell her. She's probably down by the lake. Great place to go when you want to clear your head."

"You're right. That's exactly what I'll do."

"Then you best get going."

It didn't take me long to find her. Just as Hattie had guessed, Diane was standing by the lake feeding the ducks. Not wanting to scare her off, I watched her for several moments before I made my presence known. It never ceased to amaze me the affect she had on me. After all we'd been through; she still possessed the power to render me speechless. She had the aura that commanded respect, the respect of a proud woman, yet at the same time, there was something profoundly soft and vulnerable about her. I loved the contour of her face with its keen features and her mocha chocolate skin. There was no question about it, hair or no hair, Diane was the most beautiful woman I'd ever known. I had to convey that to her. I had to let her know that her inner strength combined with her physical and spiritual beauty was absolutely radiant.

A small twig snapped under my shoe as I started walking toward her. She suddenly turned around as I approached her. "Jesus, Jacc. You scared the living daylights out of me. What are you doing sneaking up on me like that?"

"I'm sorry. I didn't mean to scare you."

"Well, you did. Heck, I thought you might have been some lunatic out to do me in."

"Diane, you know I wouldn't let anything happen to you. That's why I came looking for you. I was worried. Why did you run off?" She turned back to the ducks.

"Life's so simply for the animals. They don't worry about anything. They simply live off their instincts."

"Diane, I—"

"Jacc, you don't have to say anything."

"But I want to tell you how beautiful you look." She turned and looked at me. "Y-you mean it?" Her eyes searched mine. "Yes, I do. You're absolutely gorgeous. I was shocked when I saw you, so shocked I was speechless. I love the hair, Diane. It looks natural, so real. The style suits you perfectly." Her face lit up like a Christmas tree as she threw her arms around me. "Oh, Jacc, thank you! I was terrified you wouldn't like it. Your opinion means a lot to me. I know you wouldn't just tell me something to make me feel good. You'd be honest with me, if you thought it looked stupid or fake."

"Diane, trust me there is nothing stupid or fake about you. Wig or no wig, you are absolutely beautiful inside and out. I mean that with all my heart."

Our lips locked into a sensuous kiss before we finally pulled back. "Let's head back to the camp. Hattie needs all the help she can get. She really wants to make this a special day for Papa Joe."

"All right, Jacc, you lead the way." Arm in arm, we walked back to the campsite.

"There you are! Ya'll made it back just in time," Papa Joe said when we finally reach the camp. Hattie was just about to send out the search party for ya!"

"Don't worry, Papa Joe," I said as we walked past him, "we wouldn't have missed this shindig for anything in the world." Diane walked over to a table and began helping Clarice as I headed in Hattie's direction. "Thanks," I said once I reached her. "Aww, it was nothing. You two straighten things out?"

I smiled. "Yes, as a matter of fact, we did."

"Good," Hattie winked. "Glad to hear that. Now let's get this party started!"

As Hattie commanded, everyone began doing their part in helping with the preparations. Keith and Daryl began cleaning the fish, while Papa Joe grabbed an old newspaper. Twisting a couple sheets of the paper, he lit it with Daryl's cigarette lighter before handing the paper to me to ignite the fire in the barbeque grills. We'd decided to use two grills; one for the fish and the other for the potatoes Diane and Clarice had cut up. After all, it wouldn't be a real fish fry without french-fries. By the time all the preparations were finished we'd put together a nice spread of food consisting of fried breaded fish, tartar sauce, french-fries, coleslaw, lemon slices, potato pancakes, and lemon ice tea to wash everything down. With the all the preparations completed, everyone basically began to eat at their own leisure. Hattie outdid herself in preparing the fish. I couldn't remember when I'd eaten such delicious tasting vertebrates. In fact, the entire spread was nice. Papa Joe was pleased as well. It was a perfect way to celebrate his birthday. He complimented Hattie several times throughout the evening for putting it all together.

Daryl turned on his boom box. Everyone was enjoying themselves as we sat around laughing and reminiscing about the good old days. Even the children were having a good time running around and playing. "Ah, this is a cut!" Stretched out on a blanket with Clarice, Daryl suddenly stood up as Marvin's Gayle's Got To Give It Up blared from the boom box. Reaching down, he pulled Clarice up. "Come on, baby, dance with me." Shy and nervous, she looked around.

"Go on, Child," Hattie coaxed. "Don't just stand there, dance with the man!" Turning back to Daryl, Clarice watched him for a few seconds before she found her own rhythm. Before long she was having the time of her life as she grooved and jammed right alongside with him. We were all happy to see her just let go and really enjoy herself. Her smile was the brightest it had ever been. Taking their cue, Papa Joe and Hattie stood up to dance. Deciding we didn't want to be left out of the fun, Diane and I also joined in and began dancing to the music. After all, it was a party and we were definitely in the mood to celebrate. We danced to song after song until I practically wore down the soles of my shoes.

Needing to take a break, I walked over to a bench and sat down. Keith, who was more than happy to pick up where I'd let off, joined Diane as she continued to groove. I was glad to see she was really enjoying herself. Like Clarice, she'd been through her own personal hell. It was a wonder she hadn't had her own mental breakdown. I thanked God he'd fortified her soul with the amazing inner strength that kept her mentally strong and healthy.

Smiling, I continued to watch Diane and Keith until

something caught my eye. I froze as I stared at an obituary page from the leftover newspaper Papa Joe had used earlier. Picking up the paper from off the ground, I stared at the photo before reading the text below it.

Longtime Barrington resident Charles H. Ford
of Charles Ford Builders died Friday at
Good Samaritan Hospital after suffering a
massive heart attack. He was 62.

No, it couldn't be. The shock and realization of what I'd just read momentarily paralyzed me as I stared at my father's photo. Dead, my father was dead! My eyes quickly scanned the paper, searching for its publication date. What I saw was even more shocking. Last month's date was printed at the top of the page. *My God, he died a month ago*, I thought, my hands shaking as I held the newspaper.

"Jacc? Jacc, what's wrong? Are you all right?"
I looked up to find Diane staring at me. Her eyes were wide with worry. So engrossed in what I'd been reading, I didn't even notice the music had stopped. Everyone was now busy cleaning up the camp and getting ready to call it a night.

"I, uh, I, it's nothing just something I read."

'It's doesn't look like it's nothing to me. It's obviously upset you. Your hands are trembling. What's wrong? Let me see." Stepping closer, Diane reached for the newspaper just as I securely tucked it under my arm.

"Diane, really, it's nothing but a bunch of rhetoric about the economy starting to rebound." I hated lying to her, but what choice did I have? It was bad enough finding out this way that my father had died, but to have to talk about the lousy relationship we had was just too painful. I needed time to absorb the shock of it all and make sense of these unfortunate turn of events. I also had to figure out what I was going to do.

"Come on, "I said, changing the subject, "let's go help the others. It's late and all I want to do right now is get some shuteye." Tossing the paper in the trash, I placed my arm around her shoulder as we strolled over to the others.

February, 1985 —

"David...David!"

"Jacc, thank God, you made it. Mom's been asking for you. Dad's in with her now. It doesn't look good. The doctor says she's taken a turn for the worse."

"I don't care what the doctor says. Mom's a fighter. The cancer hasn't got her licked. It went into remission before and it'll do it again. She's going to beat this. I know she is."

"Jacc, Dr. Young says mom just doesn't have the strength to fight it this time. She's very weak. The cancer cells have spread so rapidly, her body hasn't had time to build up a resistance."

"So, what are you saying...that we should give up and wait for her to die?"

"What I'm saying is we need to prepare ourselves for the worst."

"No, I'm not going to sit back and just wait for our mother to die. There has to be something more the doctors can do. If they can't do anything, then maybe we should think about alternative treatment."

"All that can be done has been done. Jacc, I love mom, too. I don't want to loose her either, but we—"

"Forget it, David. I refuse to believe Mom's not going to make a comeback. You'll see; she's going to have a speedy recovery. I'm going in to see her now."

"Dad, how is she?"

"She's had better days. I'll leave you two alone. I'll check on David."

"All right."

"Mom, it's me, Jacc."

"J-J-Jacc."

"Mom, don't try to talk. Just take it easy. You have to concentrate on getting better. I know you're going to pull through this. You just have to. Mom, I need you."

"J-J-Jacc."

"What is it? Do you want some water?"

"N-No. I want you to listen to me."

"I'm listening."

"J-Jacc, I don't have much time. Y-Y-You have to accept the fact that I'm dying. You have to let go."

"No, Mom, don't say that. I won't let you die. You can't die. You're all I have."

"J-J-Jacc, this is all God's timing. I want you to remember you'll never be alone. I'll always watch over you. And you also have David and your father."

"David and I aren't close. We haven't been since we were children. We're miles apart. We simply don't have anything in common. As for Dad, he cursed the day I was born."

"J-Jacc, I know it...it wasn't easy for you growing up with your father, but he does love you. Try to remember that. You and David are good boys. A mother couldn't have asked for more perfect sons than you both are. And you're more alike than you know. Sure, David's ambitious like your father, but he has a good heart just like you. Promise me you'll try to get to know your brother and father before it's too late. Life's short, Jacc. T-T-The time we have here on earth is precious. Y-Y-You must not let you heart become so hardened, that you cut off your family. After all, they're all you really have down here. God handpicks our family for a special reason. P-P-Promise me, Jacc. Promise me."

"Mom, I promise. I promise. Mom, did you hear me. *"Mom, Mom, Mom! Oh, God, no! Mommmm!!!!!"*

"Wake up, Jacc." Man, you're having a nightmare." I felt someone gently shove me as I opened my eyes. Papa Joe was standing over me. "Oh, I'm sorry. Was I yelling?"

"Yeah, but don't worry about it. I figure you were having a bad dream. I had to get up anyway. Need to take a leak."

"What time is it?"

"Too early to get up. I suggest you go back to sleep. It's about three in the morning. I'm going to relieve myself. My bladder needs immediate release."

I turned over and closed my eyes, but sleep evaded me. My mother's dying words played over and over in my head. Learning that my father had died a month ago from a massive heart attack had definitely come as a complete shock. It all seemed so unreal. My father had been larger than life. He'd been ruthless in the boardroom and his company Charles Ford Builders was a force to reckon with on Wall Street. Dad had earned a reputation of being a heavy hitter both professionally and personally. He was often feared and hated as well as admired and reverenced. Now he was dead. It was just so hard to believe he was actually gone. What made matters even worse was I'd failed miserably at keeping my promise to my mother.

For years I prayed for the right moment to return home, but it never came. Every time I came close to going home, the fear of rejection crept in. I just couldn't bear to see the disappointment in my family's eyes when they learned that I was an underachiever who hadn't amounted to anything. They'd view me as nothing more than a homeless bum. The thought of them being ashamed of me hurt like hell. I guess I was hoping that if enough time passed, they might not be as judgmental.

As it stood now, time had run out or had it? After all, there was still David. Maybe this was a wakeup call for me to reach out to him. Heaven only knew what he'd been going through this past month. He'd been extremely close to Dad and I'm sure he took his passing pretty hard. I knew in my heart it was what God wanted me to do. It was time for me to return home.

BEFORE I WAS BORN

Understanding My Life's Oracle

Before I was born and sent to the earth
I was blissfully happy in my heavenly turf
Then my FATHER said, come you must dwell among the living
And be a blessing in all your giving
You'll give to the homeless, the hungry, and poor
You'll give to those who earnestly knock at your door
As my FATHER was telling me my assignment
The adversary was busy formulating his plan
So when I entered the earthly land
I'd be in financial bondage and kept in confinement
But the half hasn't been told
As my story will unfold
And my destiny is revealed
Because my fate has been sealed
By my FATHER'S unchanging hand
As I dwell in the land
And when the time is right
My heavenly angels will put the enemy and his demons to flight
So that my FATHER'S will be done
Because he chartered my course before I even was born

–Jacc –

*C*hapter Seven

The next day –

"I DON'T understand, Jacc. I don't understand why you have to leave. Why can't you tell me where you're going?" I continued to pack my small duffle bag. Diane was taking my leaving hard. She had her back to me and when she turned around, her eyes held a mixture of skepticism and worry. She thought I was abandoning her. I held out my arms to her. "Diane, I have to go. I'll be back. I can't tell you where I'm going right now, but when I get back, I'll explain everything."

"So that's it. You're just going to leave. You expect me to wait for you? And how long is that going to be, Jacc? How long are you going to be gone?"

"I-I'm not sure. Probably two weeks."

"Two weeks!"

"Diane, I know you think I'm jumping ship, but honestly I'm not. There's so much I want to tell you, but I can't right now." I walked up to her and pulled her into my arms. "I'm asking you to trust me. I need you to have a little faith. Everything is going to be alright. I going to come back for you, but I need to take care of something really important. It's something I should have done years ago. Only I was too proud and stubborn, but now I have a chance to fix things. Things have a way of coming full circle. It's time for healing.

In order for that to happen, God needs for me to trust him as I'm asking you to trust me." She pulled out of my arms. "I trust you. Promise me you'll be careful, promise me." Where had I heard that request before? An image of my mother suddenly flashed before me as I stared deep into Diane's eyes.

"I promise."

"You'd better. I want you back safe and sound. You hear me?"

"Yes, ma'am, I hear you. In fact, let's meet exactly two weeks from today at the same park we stopped by after we left Lower Wacker Drive. Meet me there at twelve noon. I'll be waiting for you at the exact spot where we ate our dinner. I promise."

"I'm going to hold you to your promise, Jacc. I'll be there waiting for you in two weeks. Do you have enough money for your trip? I can give you the rest of what I have."

"No, you keep it. You might need it. I have enough to make my trip and return. I'd better get going. I have a long journey ahead of me." I kissed her on the forehead and hoisted the duffle bag on my shoulder. For a fleeting moment, a forlorn feeling came over me, as if it was the last time I'd see her. As quickly as it surfaced, it vanished. I dismissed it as nonsense. As far as I was concerned, it would take a legion of demons to keep me from returning to Diane. Not only was I coming back for her, I was going to get her off of the streets.

No more was she going to have to live like a social outcast. It was not only time for healing, but it was also time for blessings as well. The magnitude of what God was calling me to do finally hit home. For the first time in my life, I knew I had a real purpose, a purpose that was going to have an impact on not only Diane and myself, but the millions of hurting, lost, souls. Souls who felt like God had forgotten about them. They needed to know that they weren't forgotten, that there was indeed a place on this earth they could call home. As sure as I felt there was a God in heaven, I was sure of what my purpose and my calling was. I knew time was of the essence because that familiar sense of urgency was stronger than ever.

Giving Diane a kiss goodbye, I turned and started walking away. "Jacc, wait!" I stopped and turned around.

"I love, you." Dropping my duffle bag, I ran into her inviting arms. Our lips locked in an intense kiss that left us both breathless when we finally separated. "I have to go."

"I know." Her eyes spoke volumes as we stared at each other. Finally breaking the trance, I touched her cheek and walked away.

The depth of her eyes and the message they conveyed were still etched in my mind as I sat on the commuter train several hours later. The train was heading toward Barrington, Illinois, a northwestern suburb that had a population of over

10,000. My family had called Barrington home for as long as I could remember. My parents had bought their first home in the picturesque village with its meticulously maintained houses, charming waterfront settings, and plush landscapes. When David was born, dad decided to sell our house and have an eight bedroom, six-bathroom mansion built completely from the ground up for my mother. The house is nestled on fifteen rolling and wooded acres in Barrington's more affluent community. It was in this house that I'd spent most of my childhood and it was this house that I was returning to after thirteen long years.

"Now approaching Barrington. Barrington will be our next stop." The conductor walked through the commuter car. I quickly grabbed my bag from the overhead rack and followed him as the train gradually slowed down and came to a halt. Sliding open the metal door, he stepped aside and allowed passengers to file out of the train.

The majority of the people headed to their cars or they got into the passenger side of cars waiting for them. There was no one waiting for me, no fanfare, or concerned loved one standing by to take me home. I walked down the lonely platform toward the train station and chuckled at my own foolishness. What did I expect? It wasn't like anyone knew I was coming, and even if they did, did I expect them to welcome me with some type of celebration? After all, I'm the estranged son of the late Charles Ford, the prodigal son who more or less had been nonexistent. I might as well get over myself because no one was going to reverence me like I was Christ himself returning from the dead.

Glad to see there was a small convenience store inside the train station, I walked in. "Excuse me, can I get change for a dollar?" A small framed man wearing wire rim glasses looked up from the newspaper he was reading.

"Sure." He opened his cash register and placed four quarters on the counter. I scooped up the change and placed a dollar bill down. "Thanks."

"No problem. If you're looking for a payphone, it's over there. You can also find the number to a taxi posted on the bulletin board right next to the phone."

I smiled at the man. "That's exactly what I was looking for." Walking over to the phone, I copied down the cab number, and called a taxi." Fifteen minutes was the turnaround time the dispatcher gave me over the phone. In fifteen minutes I would be on my way to finalize the last leg of my journey home. "You might as well have a cup of java, sonny. Here, it's on the house." The old man held out a Styrofoam cup. The aroma from the steaming hot liquid beckoned me as I gladly accepted his generosity. "Thanks, I could use some Joe."

"Yeah, I figured you could. The name's Jack, what's yours?" I almost choked on the coffee when I heard him mention my name. "M-My name's Jack, too. Only I spell it J-a-c-c. It's short for Jaccson."

"Well, I'll be. You don't say. I knew there was something about you when you walked in here. What brings you out this way? I've never seen you before. I know all the locals around these parts."

"Let's just say I'm on a serious mission that's long overdue."

"Better late than never."

"Yeah, you're—" The taxi suddenly pulled up and blew his horn.

"Looks like your ride's here."

"Thanks again, for the coffee." I grabbed my bag and headed out the door. "Where to?" the driver asked when I climbed into the back of his cab. "I want to go to 7755 Orchard Valley Rd."

"You got it." Adjusting his meter, he pulled off. As I sat back and watch the endless stream of black top swish by from the back seat of the taxi, I wondered how David would receive me. He might be married with children for all I knew. The thought of being an uncle had never crossed my mind. How would he explain to his family that he has a brother who he hasn't seen in thirteen years? I'm sure there will be lots of questions. Like where have I been? Why haven't I tried to call? What had I been doing all these years? Now that it was down to the wire, I realized my sudden reappearance into David's life was going to come as both a shock to him and his possible family.

Putting the shock aside, I was praying their hearts would be warm and big enough to embrace me.

"Do I make the turn here?" The driver asked as he approached a long curvy drive way. "Yes, just follow it all the way up to the house." The house could be seen through the trees as the driver steered the cab down the paved black top. He finally stopped in front of the majestic building with a terrace and entrance that led up to a pair of elegant double doors. "Here we are. That'll be twelve dollars." Reaching over the front seat, I paid him and got out.

"Thanks." He drove off as I made my way up the mounting stairs. Not wanting to prolong another minute, I rang the doorbell. As I waited for someone to answer, I looked around. The house was even larger than I'd remembered. What is it they say about out of sight, out of mind? Time definitely had a way of erasing details from your memory. Suddenly one of the double doors opened. An older Italian woman, wearing a maid's uniform, stood in the doorway. The expression on her face boldly said, *whatever you're selling, we're not buying.* "Can I help you?"

"Hi, I'm here to see Mr. Ford…that is Mr. David Ford." The woman continued to look at me as if I were wasting her time. "Is Mr. Ford expecting you?"

"N-No, he isn't."

"Then, I'm sorry he's not available." She started to close the door, but thanks to my quick reflexes, I stuck my foot into it, preventing it from closing. "Look, I know you think I'm a sales person, but I'm not. Mr. Ford's not expecting me because he hasn't seen me in a long time. If you'll just tell him Jacc's here to see him. Please, I've traveled a long way." My last comment must have appealed to her conscious because she opened the door and allowed me to step into the immaculately white marbled foyer. "Wait right here, I'll get Mr. Ford." She hurried up the curved staircase. Tired of feeling like a stranger in the house I'd grown up in, I ignored the housekeeper's request and ventured into the great room.

Keeping in fashion with the house's impeccable taste, the great room was nothing short of spectacular. It showcased expensive leather furniture that surrounded a floor-to-ceiling fireplace. A huge portrait of my father hung above it. In fact, family photos were displayed throughout the entire room. I walked over to a wall unit and picked up one of the photos. It was a picture of me as a young boy. I stared at the lad's face and wondered if there were still traces of him in me.

"J-Jacc, is it really you?" Clumsily placing the photo back on the shelf, I turned around and faced a tall, lean man dressed in a pair of Dockers and a Polo shirt. The years had been kind to him. He pretty much looked the same with the exception of the gray hair starting to show at his temples. He stared at me in disbelief. "Yeah, David, it's really me."

The years between us suddenly vanished as our eyes held each other and his facial expression went from shock and disbelief, to finally acceptance.

"My God, you've come home." The housekeeper suddenly rushed into the room. "I'm sorry, Mr. Ford, I told the man to stay put. He's disap—" Her eyes instantly shot daggers at me. "So there you are."

"It's all right, Rosa. This is my brother."

"Your brother?" She looked stunned. "Y-You mean the young man you've been searching for?" Glad to hear that David had been trying to find me, I smiled. "Yes, Rosa. I'm the long lost brother who's returned from the dead. You can relax now. I promise not to run off with the silver."

"Jesus, Jacc, that's not funny. I've searched high and low for you. I even hired a private investigator."

"Sorry, David, I knew my returning would come as a shock, but I hadn't anticipated on being treated like a stranger."

David turned to Rosa. "That'll be all. Tell cook to set another setting for dinner."

"Mamma Mia," she uttered as she took one last look at me and left the room. "Do you want a drink?" David headed toward the miniature bar.

"No, I'm not much of a drinker."

"Neither am I. I usually just have a glass of wine at dinner, but I need a stiff one after this revelation." He poured himself a shot of brandy and drank it down straight. I walked over to an enormous leather chair and sat down. I remember it was Dad's favorite chair. I'd often find him sleeping in the chair in the morning when I'd come downstairs for breakfast. He'd apparently been catching up on some reading the previous night and had fallen asleep.

"David, I'm sorry I wasn't here for Dad's funeral." Placing his glass on the bar, David turned around and faced me. The pain in his face was evident as he stared me.

"When did you hear about dad's death?

"I came across a newspaper article. It said dad had a massive heart attack." David nodded. "It was sudden and unexpected. Dad was always the pillar of health. The man rarely had a cold let alone a heart condition. That must have been some old newspaper. He died a month ago."

"I'm sad to say it was. You know I would have been here sooner, had I known."

"Would you, Jacc? Would you have come if you knew he was on his deathbed? Or would you have waited for the old man to die then show up to rub it in? Why have you come back, Jacc? Why now of all the times to just show up? Why Jacc, why?" David's eyes were filled with pent up anger from years of unanswered questions. The sad reality was I knew he was justified in his anger. There had been no excuse for me not to have contacted my dad or anyone in my family. Somehow I had to make David understand why I decided to stay away for so long.

"David, I've always felt like the black sheep in the family. As you'll recall, dad and I weren't on the best of terms when I left. He practically disowned me. He told me he wouldn't give me a dime if I dropped out of school."

"So you came crawling home now that's he's dead. You're here for the money?"

"I'm here to see if we could put the past behind us and work on being a family. I've wanted to come home for a long time, but I was afraid you'd reject me."

David walked over and sat down in the armchair across from me. "Reject you? Jacc, you rejected us. You're the one who decided to leave, remember?"

"Yeah, I remember, but that's because I knew I could never measure up to dad's expectations. David, I've been living a nomadic lifestyle. Right now I'm homeless."

The look on his face wasn't what I had expected or feared. Surprisingly disappointment and disgust weren't visible in his eyes. What was present was shock and sheer disbelief. It was obvious he didn't know how to react to what I'd just told him.

"Say what? Jacc, run that by me again."

"I said I'm homeless."

"As in dirty-bum-on-the-street homeless?"

"That's a stereotype. All homeless people aren't dirty bums, but, yes, to answer your question, I'm living on the street." David ran his fingers through his hair as the reality of what I'd said finally hit home. "My God, Jacc, how long have you been homeless?" I got up and walked over to the wall unit. I picked up a photo of dad. It was still hard to believe that he was dead. Placing the photo back on the shelf, I turned to David. "I've been homeless just a little shy of a year."

"Jesus, Jacc, how the hell do you survive on the streets?"

"You'd be surprised the survival skills people develop when it becomes a do or die situation." I walked back to my father's favorite chair, sat down, and looked David straight in the eyes. "Can you see why I hesitated about coming home? Dad's always been disappointed in me. This news would have only solidified his opinion of my failed life."

"No, Jacc, I don't understand. You said you've been homeless for almost a year, but you've been gone for thirteen. What have you been doing during all that time?"

"I mainly worked odd jobs before landing a job with a manufacturing company. They produced wall units and cabinets. I worked there for seven years until I was laid off last year."

"Okay, so you lost your job. Get up and get another one. Jacc, that doesn't justify living on the street. It's the lowest a man can ever go. I don't understand how you can give up on yourself. I don't get it. What's really going on? Are you on drugs or something? If so, we can get you some help. Get you into rehab."

David's questions and attitude didn't surprise me. I didn't expect him to be any different from those who associated homelessness to the individual's own lack of effort. It just never occurred to people that homelessness was a greater problem than what they assumed. "It's been hard trying to find work. Many companies are moving their operations oversees. I know you think I came back for the money, and in a way, its truth. I came back to ask if you can float me a loan. I just need enough to invest in a project I've been contemplating."

I held my breath as I waited for David to respond. Everything was riding on his answer. I knew it was a long shot. After all, he had no earthy reason to believe me, let alone trust me. Not that I'd ever given him reason not to, but I could see where he might be skeptical about my motives. After all, I've made no effort to contact him in thirteen years and I just show up at his doorstep after learning my father had died. David got up and poured himself another drink. Taking his glass to his lips, he tossed the liquid to the back of his throat in one shot and cringed as the strong spirit rushed down like a raging fire. Not knowing how to interpret his stall tactic, I silently prayed as I held my head down and stared at my hands.

"Jacc, you don't need me to float you any money. Hell, you have enough money to do whatever you want to do. You're a rich man."

"Wh-whaat?" I looked up to find David staring at me. I searched his face for some inkling that he was putting me on, but there was none. Getting up, I walked over to my brother and looked him dead in the eyes. "I-I don't understand, David. You're joking, because if you're not, then what the hell are you talking about?"

"Jacc, I'm serious. You're filthy rich. I know you think dad cut you out of the will, but he didn't. As the eldest son, he left you controlling interest in the family business. Everything's tied up in probate. Dad held out hope you'd come back someday. He loved you. It broke his heart when you left. There wasn't a day that went by that he didn't think about you. Day after day, month after month, year after year, he'd have cook set a place for you at the dinner table. He'd stare at the empty dining room chair where you used to sit. It was as if he expected you to walk in any minute and take a seat, but you never did. Being a proud man, he never mentioned he regretted that stupid argument you two had, but I know he did. I could see it in his eyes when he thought no one was looking. Then one day, he announced he was going to try and find you. He hired a team of private investigators. For years dad search and searched for you, yet nothing was panning out, until we got a call from someone who claimed they knew where you were." Sitting up straight, I listened as David continued.

"Both dad and I flew to California to meet the person who'd made the claims. As it turned out, they were trying to extort money from us. They're now serving time in jail. When dad grew too weary to continue the search, I hired my own team of PIs."

"Wow, that's some story. I never figured anyone was looking for me. It never crossed my mind that dad would have spent years trying to find me. We had some pretty heated words the day I left. I figured he'd really washed his hands of me. I've spent years reliving that day in my mind and regretting every word I said. I guess pride has stopped me from contacting dad as well as embarrassment. Learning he was trying to find me is incredible. I wish I'd known how he really felt. It would have saved all of us a lot of pain and lost time."

"Yes, it would have. We can't change the past, Jacc, what's done is done. The only thing we can do is try to reestablish a relationship with each other. Both mom and dad would have wanted that."

"I agree, David. Before mom died, she made me promise to try and establish a relationship with you and dad. I feel so guilty because I didn't make good on my promise to her. It's haunted me for years."

"It's not too late, Jacc. You've come home. That's a major step. We have all the time there is to catch up."

Just as I was about to comment, Rosa entered the room. Quietly closing the door behind her, her eyes briefly shifted to me before she gave David her full attention.

"Pardon me for interrupting, Mr. Ford, but cook is ready to serve dinner.

Standing up, Davie smiled. "Thank you, Rosa. Tell cook we'll be right out."

"As you wish, sir." She threw me another glance before she left. It was obvious she still had her guard up. Apparently, David noticed her reaction as well. "I wouldn't

worry about, Rosa. She can be a little protective at times."
Getting up, I followed David out of the room. "That's understandable. I'm sure she's curious about all of this. After all, a strange man shows up and claims to be her boss's long lost brother. It has the making for an intriguing mystery novel."

The dinning room table was set for two with imported dinnerware and goblets. I sat down in the seat where I'd sat for years. Everything seemed familiar, yet surprisingly odd. I never thought I'd actually step foot back inside this house least of all be sitting here having dinner with my brother. Taking his seat, David waited until we were served before he raised his glass and made a toast.

"To my brother, Jacc. May he have a bright future. Welcome home." Lifting up my glass, I toasted David's sentiments.

Cook had prepared a delicious meal consisting of tender mouthwatering pot roast, steamed white rice, potatoes and carrots along with tossed salad. Topping off the meal was an expensive bottle of imported Bordeaux wine.

During the course of the meal, David and I talked about what had been going on with him since I'd left.

"I finished college with a Master's Degree. I finally took over running Charles Ford Builders two years ago, however, dad still called a lot of the shots behind the scenes. It was almost as if he'd never retired. After all he was still an active board member with controlling interest. Although his death came as a shock to his friends and family, it was viewed as a window of opportunity for his foes. Right now I'm in a battle with one of dad's staunch competitors. They're trying to stage a hostile takeover by gaining controlling interest. I've been able to keep the vultures at bay so far, but I'm just not sure how long I'll be able to prevent a takeover. There's talk that some of the other shareholders are considering selling their shares. My shares alone aren't enough to allow me controlling interest."

David took a sip of wine before he continued. "The fact that dad named you in his will as the recipient of his shares makes it difficult for the shares to be transferred to me. I'd have to prove you're officially dead otherwise your assets continue to remain tied up in probate. I never gave up looking for you, Jacc. In fact my PI is stilling trying to find you. Dad left his shares to you because he never gave up hope that you'd come back one day and rightfully claim your stake in the company."

As I listened to my brother, I thought about my father's desire to keep the business within the family. It was never his intention to have the company break up and be sold off. He'd built Charles Ford Builders into the corporate giant it was today. I'm sure he was turning over in his grave at the very thought of letting it fall into the hands of someone who wasn't his heirs.

The more I thought about it, the angrier I became. There was no way in hell I was going to dishonor dad's memory by letting the company be stolen from right under our noses. I owed it to him. We may have had our differences, but he was still my father. Picking up my napkin, I wiped the corners of my mouth before laying it on the plate.

"David, they're not going to win. I owe it to dad to do all I can to prevent it. He worked hard his whole life to accomplish his dream. CFB is his legacy and it's going to remain in this family for the next generation of Fords. Timing is everything. I'd say I came home just in the nick of time. There's about to be a major shakeup with the shareholders."

The grin on David's face and the look in his eyes said it all. I knew he was right there with me. "You're right, Jacc, it's all about timing. A monkey wrench is about to be thrown into their plans. The fallout definitely isn't going to be pretty."

I MET A MAN

A Tailor Made Man

I met a man who made me Smile
If only for a little While
I met a man who brought me Joy
For he was truly the real McCoy
He was strong and Masculine
Never shy and Coy
I met a man who was tailor-made for Me
He made my spirit radiate with Glee
I met a man God Chose
Because he knows what's Best
I can Attest
Now we're far Apart
And it's tearing at my Heart
Yes, I met a man who made me Smile
If only for a little While

−Diane −

C*hapter Eight*

"HOW is she doing, Hattie?"

"The same, Keith. It's been a couple of days since he left and she's still moping around like she lost her best friend. You sure he's coming back?"

"Yeah, that's what Jacc said. I don't know why Diane thinks he's not going to honor his word? He's never lied to her before."

"Hand me that towel over there so I can wipe my hands, will ya? Thanks. It stands to reason why she doesn't believe him. No one saw this coming. One day we were all celebrating Papa's Joe's birthday and the next day Jacc ups and announces he's leaving. To make matters worse, he doesn't tell anybody where he's going or how long he'd be gone."

"Actually, he did say he'd be back in two weeks."

"Did he say where he was going?"

"No, just said he had to take care of something very important. Jacc loves Diane. He'd never abandon her like that. He'll be back, watch and see."

"I sure hope you're right. Breakfast is just about ready. How about going to fetch Diane? She took the children down to the lake for an early morning swim."

"All right, I'll go round everyone up."

"Here, take this apple. That ought to hold you until you get back. It's a wonder I have any bacon left. You thought I didn't see you sneaking a couple of strips when my back was turned."

"Hahaha, I guess I'm busted. Thanks, Hattie, this apple will definitely hold me. I'll be back soon."

"Bones, James, and Thomas, come on out of the water! It's time we started heading back. Hattie's just about finished making breakfast!"

"All right, Diane, we're coming! Give us a few minutes to dry off and get dressed!"

"Diane, you want me to wake up, Amanda?"

"No, leave her be, Keith. She looks so peaceful sleeping on that blanket. You can get her up when we're just about to leave."

"Okay. How are you holding up?"

"I'm okay, I guess. I just don't get it, Keith. What would make him take off like that?"

"I don't know, Diane. Jacc didn't tell me anything other than something urgent came up. Maybe it had to do with his family."

"Jacc didn't talk much about his family. He only mentioned them once and that was to say there was distance between them. Funny how you think you know a person then you realize you really don't know them at all. Think about it. What do any of us really know about each another? Like whom are we supposed to get in contact with if something should ever happen one of us?"

"I can't answer that, Diane, but if you think that's something to ponder, here's another question. If the homeless really had someone to call, then why the hell are they homeless in the first place? I know you and Jacc feel it's all about economics. I don't dispute that, but I think the problem ultimately starts with people being disconnected from their families. Families today are extremely dysfunctional. They just don't stick together like they did in the old days. Family unity is practically nonexistent. Things have deteriorated to the point where people are living in the same city as their kinfolk, yet they don't speak to them much less see them for years."

"That's true, Keith. In today's society it's all about individualism. Families in general are less clannish than they used to be. They've taken the attitude that they don't owe each other anything. You know the 'I'm not my brother's keeper' type of mentality. Families don't feel obligated to each other. People in general feel like they had to struggle to get where they are so it's expected that everyone has to struggle to obtain their own goals. It's the process of paying your dues. Nobody owes you anything in life. I've learned that all too well. It was instilled in me from a very early age by my own family."

"Diane, I know exactly what you're talking about. I think a lot of us have booshie relatives. My family can't stand to see me coming. They act like they're afraid I'm going to either hit them up for some money or I'm going to ask to stay with them. That's why I don't turn to them. I've basically been on my own since I was a kid. I can remember sleeping under porches and in abandoned buildings as a child. My mother died when I was thirteen. I come from a large family, but they really didn't want to be bothered with me and my four brothers so we were placed in foster homes. The foster parents were only using us for the monthly check. There wasn't any real love in the home. I remember I kept running away. I often found myself sleeping in condemned buildings. Technically I've been homeless ever since I was thirteen. When a person says nobody owes you anything they're basically telling you not to ask them for anything because they don't want to extend their hand. If you were told that as a child, Diane, it's understandable why you're as independent and as strong as you are. You took what was told to you to heart and you learned not to depend on anyone. I was also made to feel like I shouldn't reach for my family and I don't."

"Keith, do you suppose that's why Jacc's been as distant and cut off from his family?"

"It's hard to say. Like you said, he never opened up about his family or his past. I'll say this though; he doesn't come across as the kind of person that's lived the hardcore street life. He doesn't have that rough edge persona like most guys who've been on the trail for a long time. I actually know a guy who told me he's been homeless for thirty years. Heck, if there was a homeless pension fund, he'd definitely qualify for it."

"My God, Keith, I can't even imagine spending thirty years being homeless. As hard as it is to believe, I know it's true. It's so sad the way people have fallen through the cracks because they don't have a strong connection to their families. Hey, guys! Come on; let's put a move on it! Hurry up!"

"Keith, I remember when my family would have these huge family reunions. I was a little girl and I always felt a great sense of pride in knowing I was part of a magnificent and diverse group of people. From my immediate family to my extended one, they were a cast of characters that promoted black pride and family unity. Somewhere along the way my family stopped promoting these concepts. The sad reality is unity has always been the furthest from everyone's mind. When you're a child your prospective is very different concerning the world and the people around you. As I grew older, I began to realize the dynamics of what was really going on in my family. They aren't any different from millions of other families in the world. They have secrets and skeletons they'd prefer to stay buried. They're also jealous, competitive, disloyal, and dysfunctional like a lot of people. They aren't immune to drug addiction and alcoholism nor are they the Huxtables and although some of them are scholars; all of them aren't academic achievers who go on to college. Some of them are incarcerated while some are deeply religious, and others don't believe in God at all. I come from a typical black family that's capable of love as well as afflicting pain on each other. Keith, when you say I took to heart what was instilled in me as a young girl, you're right. I had no choice. Thinking back, I don't harbor bitterness toward my family. I do at times feel sad that we aren't close, that we can't truly be accepting of one another with all of our shortcomings."

"Yeah, Diane, forgiveness and acceptance are easier said than done. If people would just learn to accept each other for who they are and not try to hold them to their own expectations then life would be a whole lot easier. Speaking of forgiveness, Hattie is never gonna forgive us if we keep holding up breakfast. I'll get Amanda."

"Hey, ya'll, we're leaving! Let's go, now!"

"Say, Diane, is Jacc ever gonna come back? It seems like he's been gone forever."

"Bones, it's been a week since he left. As far as I know, he's supposed to return next week."

"Gee, I hope next week hurries up and gets here cause I sure do miss him."

"Me too. Say, why don't you draw him a picture since you have all your art supplies spread out on the picnic table? You can give it to him when he gets back. I'm sure he'd love it."

"Thanks, Diane, that's a neat idea. I'm gonna draw him a real nice one!"

"Who are you gonna draw a picture for, Bones?"

"Keith, Bones is making a picture for Jacc."

"You don't say. These are really good. Bones, you're a natural born artist."

"Thanks, Keith. Do you think Jacc will like it?"

"Are you kidding? He'll love it. I'll let you get back into your creative zone."

"Diane, I'm glad to see you're feeling better about Jacc. I know you were worried that he might be gone for good."

"Actually, I'm very worried, but I didn't want to let on to Bones that I am. What if Jacc decides not to come back or worse what if something happens to him that prevents him from coming back? I've been frantic with worry everr since he left. I wish he'd confided in me before he decided to leave. You know if he decides not to return, it wouldn't be the first time a man runs off and leaves the woman behind. Keith, I've always prided myself on having a level head. Realistically, a girl can't expect to find a stable man on the trail. Being homeless has a way of tearing at a man's sense of stability. Women have a hard enough time finding a man who isn't afraid of commitment. Looking for stability in a homeless man, who's used to drifting from place-to-place is a stretch. Maybe Jacc realized he wanted to bail out before things started getting too serious with us. Not sure how to tell me, he just decided to leave."

"Diane, you and I both know Jacc's not like that. He isn't the kind of man who'd skip out on a woman. Sure, being homeless a man learns to live by his instincts and he does become accustomed to living a nomadic lifestyle, but that doesn't mean he's not going to stick by those he cares about. Don't let this incident cloud your judgment about Jacc. He loves you. If he said he's coming back, then he will. I've never met a more honorable man than Jacc. He's not going to abandon you, why would he? He's stuck by you this far and he's going to continue to do so. Trust me you guys will be together again. "

"Keith, I sure hope you're right. I know Jacc's a good man. It's one of the things I love most about him. He's very respectful and loyal. I just wish I knew what it was that compelled him to leave."

"Hopefully he'll confide in you when he returns. You've only got one more week to go. You guys are meeting at the park downtown right?"

"You better believe I'll be there. Jacc wants to meet at noon. It'll take a herd of wild bulls to keep me from showing up. I just hope I'm not disappointed. I love Jacc. If we're going to be together, I have to trust him."

"That's right. I just don't see him standing you up. He's probably missing you just as much as you're missing him."

"If he is then I hope he cuts his trip short because I want my Jacc back."

"Hey, Keith, Diane, look, I'm all finished."

"Wow, Bones. It's really nice. I love the colors."

"You really like it, Diane?"

"Sure, do. And I know Jacc will too. Why don't you put it inside your folder so it won't get ruined? That way it'll be in a safe place."

"Good idea. I'll put it right here. I'll see ya'll later. I'm gonna go find Daryl and see how many fish he's caught so far. Maybe he caught a big one like I did."

"All right, Bones. Have fun."

"Bones, boy, where were you? We've been looking all over the place for ya."

"Aww, shucks, Hattie, you don't have to look so mad. I was just talking with Keith and Diane. I figured ya'll knew I was with them and that I'd meet you down here by the lake."

"Boy, we ain't no mind readers. How the heck are we supposed to know you were with Diane and Keith?"

"Cause I just told you."

"You getting smart with her, boy?"

"No sir, Papa, Joe."

"Good, cause I don't like young folks talking back to their elders. That's not how things are done down south."

"Yes, sir."

"You say you were with Diane and Keith?"

"That's right. They're back at the camp. Me and Diane was drawing some pictures. I made one for Jacc. I can't wait till he comes back."

"I'm sure Diane can't wait either."

"Hattie, what I don't understand is why he left in the first place? Don't seem right a man just up and run off, leaving his woman. Don't tell her nothing, where he's going or exactly when he's gonna be back."

"You're right, Papa Joe, it ain't right, but I suppose Jacc's got his reasons. It must have been something real important for him to run off like he did. I'd sure like to know what it is, but I reckon all any of us can do is wait for him to come back and tell us. According to Diane, he's due back next week. Joe, you better never run off on me. I'll put up with a lot of things, but I positively ain't gonna stand for no desertion. You hear me?"

"I hear ya, Hattie. You ain't got to worry. We've gone through too much together. I ain't going anywhere. You're stuck with me."

"Glad to hear it. Now let's go see what Daryl has in that bucket. Come on, Bones, let's go help Daryl catch some more fish!"

"I'll be right there, Papa Joe. Gotta get my fishing pole."

"I swear that child has too much energy. Come on, Joe, no need wasting the rest of the afternoon dillydallying around. There's fish to be caught."

WHAT SHE MEANS TO ME

A Love To Cherish

What she means to me
Can't be expressed in mere words you see
The beautiful woman of color
I wouldn't trade for any other
She's truly a special woman
Who's been included in my life's plan
She's been an inspiration to me
Through her inner strength that's transparent for all
to see
She's strived hard all her life
I'd be proud to call her my wife
She's smart and wise
With a rambunctious laugh that's a wonderful
surprise
What she means to me
Can't be expressed in mere words you see

–Jacc –

*C*hapter Nine

"LET ME get this straight. You're Charles Ford eldest son?"

"That's correct."

"You'll forgive me if I'm skeptical, but given the nature of what's at stake, it seems reasonable to question the validity of your claim."

"Mr…ur…Donavan, correct?"

"That's right."

"Mr. Donavan, I can appreciate your honesty, but frankly, I don't give a damn if you're skeptical or not. The fact is I am Charles Ford's oldest son, Jaccson Ford. Yes, there's a lot at stake meaning the inheritance my father left behind and the future of his company. Being an intelligent man as I'm sure you are; you certainly don't think I came down to your office unprepared. I have all the necessary documents to prove my identity. DNA tests can also be provided. My brother and I have discussed it and we're prepared to have my father's body exhumed if need be. Don't get me wrong, I understand you're just doing your job as the legal executor of my father's estate, but we're talking about a time sensitive issue. Charles Ford Builders is going through a critical phase right now. My father's death has shaken things up amongst the shareholders and unfortunately the company's competitors."

"Mr..uh..Ford—"

"Call me Jacc."

"Very well, Jacc, I'm aware of the possible takeover the company is facing. As the legal executor of Charles Ford estate, I make it my business to keep abreast of all matters concerning his assets. I've been working closely with the probate court to legally find a way for Mr. Ford's assets to be transferred over to David. Although Mr. Ford left David a substantial amount of money along with other valuable assets, he left the bulk of his fortune to his oldest son, which is rather peculiar given the nature of their stained relationship. For the sake of the argument, let's assume you're really Mr. Ford's son, why have you suddenly taken an interest in the family business? From what I understand, you've never been remotely interested in anything that had to do with the company."

"I see you've done your homework, Mr. Donavan. You're right; my relationship with my father was rather stained. I had no idea dad even included me in his will least of all he'd left me with controlling interesting in the company."

"Come on, Jacc, you expect me to believe you knew nothing about the inheritance? I doubt that. You had to have known. Why else would you have come back? What I don't understand is why Mr. Ford didn't leave David the bulk of his estate? Let's just say you hadn't come back, your father's assets would still be tied up because David has to either show proof you're no longer living in order for all the assets to be awarded to him. As the family attorney, I advised David to have you declared legally dead given the fact that no one had heard from you or seen you in over thirteen years. Everything possible was done to locate you including running legal notices in national and international newspapers."

"Yes, David told me all about his and my father's grueling search to find me."

"I see, then he must have also told you about the many crackpots who came forward claiming to either be you or know of your whereabouts. You can see why I'm cautious about your claims. David may be convinced you're real, but as the family lawyer and overseer of his father's estate, I need to be sure you're legit."

"Of course, I understand completely. As I stated, I can provide proof of my identity. In fact, everything is right here inside this folder. I'll also go ahead and start looking into having the DNA tests done. You can either contact David or myself directly if you need any more information."

"Very, well, Jacc, I'll look over your documents and make sure everything checks out. As it stands the next probate court hearing is this Friday at a 10:00 a.m. sharp. We were set to ask the judge to declare you legally dead, but it's obviously going to be put on hold until we can determine if you are indeed Charles H. Ford's legitimate son, Jaccson Ford. You'll be expected to attend the court hearing. I'll be in touch before hand if something arises or the hearing has been rescheduled."

"All right, unless I hear otherwise, I'll see you Friday. Thank you for taking the time to see me on short notice. No need to get up. I can see myself out."

Closing the door behind me, I walked to the elevator and stepped inside as its door opened. My meeting with Stan Donovan had gone as I'd expected. For the past week David had filled me in on the inner working of Donovan's mind. A longtime friend of my father's, he was as shrewd as dad and fiercely loyal to those he considered a friend. Nothing got past Donavan as it shouldn't since dad had entrusted him with handling all his legal and financial affairs. The sooner he was able to verify my identity the better. Things were moving exceeding fast. Time was definitely working against us. For the past week David had managed to keep things on an even keel with the other shareholders, but I wasn't sure how long he would be able to keep them from selling off their shares.

There were other changes that had taken place within the past week as well. I was brought on board with the company as an independent consultant. He thought it was the best way for me to get a feel of the dynamics within the company as well as observe all the game players. No one really knew my true identity as Charles Ford's oldest son.

We decided to use a fake name for the time being. I was now part of the corporate world. Dressed in a suit and tie, I headed to the office every day to learn the tricks of the trade within the organization. My father would have been proud of me if he'd been alive. David was certainly more than happy to help mold me so I could eventually take my rightful place as the heir to our father's throne. After all, I was the secret weapon he was counting on to blow his opponents' ship right out of the water. The shareholders weren't going to know what had hit them when my true identity was revealed. It was about timing and the time was drawing near. Not wanting to disappoint my brother, I paid close attention to everything and learned fast. Nothing got past me. I was as shrewd as my father when it came to discerning who people really were and just as shrewd when it came to business.

The issue for me wasn't that I couldn't measure up or handle running the business. No, that had never been the issue contrary to what my father and David thought. The truth was I simply never had the interest or the desire to fill dad's shoes. In fact, I still didn't, but for the sake of saving the company from a takeover, I was willing step into them. I knew in my heart once everything was back on track and things were once again copasetic, then I knew I was going to step back and let David shine in the area he was most comfortable with. In my opinion, dad should have given

David the controlling interest in the company instead of me. This really wasn't my arena. It wasn't, however, because I didn't fit in, to the contrary, I fit in like a hand in a glove. I had the look and image that blended in with the best of the young hotshots on Wall Street not to mention the intelligence, natural instincts, as well as savvy business sense I'd inherited from my father. Dad had known all along I was capable of taking over the helms and I guess subconsciously I'd known as well.

What dad never knew, however, was there was a greater purpose for my life that just didn't lineup with the future he so desperately wanted me to have. Heck, I didn't truly understand it myself until I actually became homeless. It was only then that I began to understand the magnitude of my calling. My reappearance back into my brother's life couldn't have come at a more crucial time. Once everything was taken care of, I was going to definitely set the wheels in motion with my plan to build homes for the homeless.

Stepping out the elevator, I strolled through the main lobby of the office complex and out onto the main street. David had insisted I either drive dad's black BMW or his Roll Royce. According to David, neither had been driven since dad's death. Not into stately cars, I decided on the black beamer. It was more befitting of the whole young successful go getter persona David wanted me to project as

I gradually assimilated back into mainstream society. It didn't take me long to reach the parking garage and collect the car. Soon I was cruising through traffic like the rest of the millions of motorists traveling here and there. As I sped down the expressway, I thought about all I'd been through and the transformation of what I was supposed to represent now.

And what a transformation it was. Here I am a homeless man now driving a very expensive car, dress in an expensive tailored suit, on my way to a mansion in Barrington, Illinois, and the woman I loved was still sleeping on the ground in the backwoods of Hammond, Indiana. There was definitely something wrong with this picture. To some it would be so easy to forget about Diane and all the homeless people I'd met while I was on the trail, but I couldn't forget about them. I could never forget about Diane, Keith, Hattie, Papa Joe, Daryl, Clarise, Bones, Little Amanda, James, and Thomas. They were my friends and Diane was the center of my joy. There wasn't a day that went by that I didn't think about her. There just wasn't any way in hell I wasn't going to go back for her. I hadn't told David about Diane or my plans, but as soon as everything was settled with the inheritance, I planned to tell him everything. Then I was going to bring Diane back to my father's estate.

I finally turned down the long driveway of my parent's estate and drove past the main house to the parking garage as the garage door automatically rose. Parking the car, I turned off the engine and got out. I could hear voices coming from the great room as I entered the house from the door that led into the kitchen.

"Good evening, sir. Dinner will be served shortly."

"Thank you, Cook. I take it we're having guests for dinner?"

"Yes, sir. Mr. Ford's fiancée, Penelope, and her close friend will be staying for dinner. Mr. Ford instructed me to prepare a special dinner to celebrate your return home after all these years."

"Well, I better go and introduce myself. I'll let David know dinner will be ready shortly."

"Thank you, sir."

"Anytime, Cook, and you don't have to call me sir. You can call me Jacc." Smiling at the older man, I walked out of the kitchen and down the long corridor to the great room. The sound of laughter could be heard coming from inside the room as I approached the door. Opening it, I walked in as David rose to his feet. "Ah, Jacc, I'm so glad you're back. Cook's preparing a very special dinner in celebration of your homecoming."

"Yes, I know. I came in through the kitchen. Cook says dinner will be ready shortly."

"Great, now, that you're here, I'd like to formally introduce you to my fiancée, Penelope Singleton." A tall, attractive blond, with shoulder length hair and green eyes, stood up. "Hello, Jacc. It's a pleasure meeting you. I've heard nothing but good thing about you from David. He's just thrilled to have you back in his life. I hope you and I will become very good friends. By the way, my friends call me Penny." Smiling, I shook her extended hand. It was obvious why David was taken with Penny. She had a warm sincere smile and a friendly air about her. On the surface, everything about her appearance gave the impression that she was a snob. However, throughout the course of the evening, I was pleasantly surprised to discover that she was anything but snobbish.

"Thank you, Penny. It's a pleasure meeting you. I'm afraid you have me at a disadvantage. David never told me he was engaged." Her eyes widened in shock before turning on David with accusation in them. "Oh, David, for heaven's sake, when were you going to tell Jacc about me, before or after the wedding? I swear you can be so forgetful!"

Laughing, David draped his arm around her shoulders. "Can you blame me for wanting to keep you a secret just a little while longer? I'm positively the luckiest man alive because I'm marrying the most beautiful woman in the world."

Talk about knowing just the right words to say, David's charm worked like magic. Turning, Penny crossed her arms around the back of his neck and planted a passionate kiss on his lips. It was obvious they were in love and they often settled their little disagreements in this manner. I was happy for David. I was glad he'd found someone to share his life with. Watching them, I thought about how it would soon be for me and Diane. Soon we'll be happily settled in our own home planning our future as I'm sure David and Penny were probably doing. "Excuse me, I hate to break up this little intimate scene, but don't you think you should at least introduce me?" Penny's friend stood up and smiled at me. Her dark brown hair was fashionably cut and her ruby red lipstick contrasted with her porcelain white skin and grey eyes. She was attractive, yet I didn't get the same sincere vibe I got from Penny. Somehow I felt her snooty image lived up to her true personality. Pulling out of each other's arms, Penny smiled as she wiped her lipstick off of David's lips. "I'm sorry," she said as she faced me and her friend, "Jacc, this is my friend Shawnee McDaniel. Shawnee, this is Jacc, a distant relative of David's."

"Well, Jacc," she purred, "It's a pleasure to meet you. I must say you're as handsome if not more handsome than David." As attractive as she was, her beauty didn't in the least bit faze me. Everything about her reminded me of my ex-girlfriend, Heather. No thanks, I'd had my share of selfish, thoughtless women who were basically looking for a trophy man with a fat bank account and a Lamborghini. Besides, if Shawnee knew the truth that I was once homeless, she'd run like a bat out of hell for the nearest exit. Deciding to play it cool for the sake of David and Penny, I smiled. "Thank you, Shawnee, I'm going to assume you meant that as a compliment to both me and David." Her eyes widened with surprise as if she hadn't expected to be put on the spot. There was a hint of indignation in them, which she quickly masked by a false air of bewilderment. "Well of course, what else would I have meant? I hope my comment didn't rub you or David the wrong way. It wasn't meant to. My apologies if I offended anyone."

"Are you kidding?" Penny came to her rescue.

"Shawnee, you couldn't offend these two even if you tried. I'm sure Jacc's skin is as tough as David's." She winked at me. Taking her cue, I decided to let Shawnee off the hook. "You're right, Penny, my skin's as tough as it comes. Shawnee, if you'll allow me to escort you to dinner, I'm sure Cook is about ready to serve."

"Good idea." David threw me a look that clearly said, *what the hell is going on*? "Penny, shall we?" Offering her his arm, he escorted her out of the room as Shawnee and I followed.

With the exception of our awkward introduction, Shawnee and I managed to be cordial and pleasant to one another throughout the course of the dinner. It certainly helped the overall atmosphere and lightened the mood drastically largely because she was being guarded and cautious about what she said. After all, she couldn't have me being too discerning and exposing her true nature.

Penny on the other hand, was lucid and easily talked up a storm. I learned she'd met David three years ago just a year before he'd actually took over the company. She'd been hired as the new marketing director and they hadn't taken to each other right away. Being the boss's son, she thought he was cocky to no end and definitely a lady's man. According to Penny, she had to fight off all of the barracudas that wanted to get their hooks into him and David didn't make the situation any better. He certainly didn't discourage them.

I laughed as I listened to Penny tell of a particular incident when she had to actually kick a woman out of his office. She'd walked in and found the woman sprawled out on his desk dressed in a scanty outfit. David hadn't arrived yet. Fuming, Penny ordered the woman to get out as she picked up a small fire extinguisher and sprayed the woman. She figured it would cool her off. David walked in and found the woman soaked to the bone. Humiliated, the woman ran out of the office and never spoke to David again.

Quite a story, it had us laughing with the exception of Shawnee. It was obvious she didn't find Penny's tale amusing. In fact, she looked bored. To be honest, I didn't really see what the connection was with her and Penny. Their personalities were as opposite as night and day. It was hard to see how they'd managed to become friends. Oh, well, it wasn't my place to judge even if it was odd.

After dinner we adjourned into the great room for an after dinner cocktail. It was obvious I wasn't going to get a chance to tell David what had transpired in Donavan's office. Deciding to fill him in first thing in the morning over breakfast, I relaxed and enjoyed the rest of the evening.

Sleep evaded me as I lay in the king size bed and listened to the ferocious wind howl outside. Diane was foremost in my mind. I prayed she was safe and warm. It was definitely not a night to be sleeping outdoors. Turning over, I tried once again to fall asleep."

"J-Jacc, are you awake?" There was a tap at the door.

"Jacc." Recognizing David's voice, I got up to open it.

"What's wrong? Has something happened?" Walking past me, David sat down in the comfortable armchair sitting near the fireplace. Logs crackled as they gradually turned to cinder and ash. Closing the door, I walked over and sat in the seat opposite him. It was late or should I say early. Glancing at the clock sitting on the nightstand, I wondered why my brother was sitting in my room at 2:00 a.m. What was so urgent that it couldn't wait until daylight? "What's going on, David? I'm assuming it's something that couldn't wait."

"Depends on how you look at it. First off, what the hell was that all about earlier? You couldn't have been any ruder to Penny's friend. Want to explain what the hell was going on there?"

"You got me up at two in the morning to discuss that Spawn woman? Geez, David, this really could have waited!"

"Her name is Shawnee, and I actually wanted to find out how things went with Donavan. This thing with Shawnee just came up because I'm confused by your reaction to her. I don't get it." Running my fingers through my hair, I sighed as I leaned back in my seat. If David couldn't see past Shawnee's fake mask, then he was really blind. "I've known women like her throughout my life. I'm sure you've come across a few of them throughout the years yourself. Penny's a wonderful woman. You're a lucky man. She'll make a good wife for you. What I don't get is the friendship she has with Shawnee or why you can't see beyond her façade?"

"Actually, I do." Surprised, I sat up and stared at him. "Run that by me again?"

"I said I see through Shawnee. Have you ever heard of keeping your friends close, but keep your enemies closer?"

"I don't follow."

"Let me explain. Shawnee is the daughter of dad's staunch enemy, Lester McDaniel of McDaniel Supply Company. She befriended Penny right after we started dating. I didn't know who she was at first and by the time I'd found out, it was too late. Penny was already taken with her. She tries to give people the benefit of doubt until they prove otherwise. If they prove to be unworthy, then watch out.

I've been on the other end of her wrath a few times. So far Shawnee's been very careful as to not tip her hand to Penny. I don't have concrete proof, but I suspect Lester McDaniel sent his daughter to befriend Penny in hopes of obtaining inside information. I'm almost sure he's the one behind the takeover. Dad never trusted him. His company was a rival of ours and they often competed with us for major contracts by trying to outbid us. The bidding wars went on for a while until McDaniel Supply was hit with mounting personal injury claims stating asbestos had been found in products they'd sold over forty years ago. The mounting litigation costs eventually forced the company to file for bankruptcy. They've shoved out millions of dollars to resolve the issue. Keep in mind this is minus what the insurance companies have been willing to pay."

Learning exactly who our opponent was certainly shed a whole new light on things. I could see why David wanted to keep Shawnee close and why he didn't want to rock the boat with her just yet. "David this is all intriguing and it certainly sheds insight into what we're up against. What's the status on McDaniel Supply right now? I'm assuming they've had all of their assets frozen and even have a corporate freeze on hiring. They probably had a bout of layoffs as well. This type of fallout is typical when a company files bankruptcy. What's puzzling is why would Lester McDaniel be trying to acquire Charles Ford Builders at this stage in the game? He's not in any position to be acquiring other companies. Expansion should be the last thing on his mind."

"That may have been true when the company first filed bankruptcy several years ago, but under the protection of Chapter 11, they've had time to reconstruct and reorganize. According to their latest press release, McDaniel Supply has emerged from bankruptcy stronger than ever. In the wake of dad's death, McDaniel feels the time is just right to make his move. He's been after the company for a long time. Expansion is very much on his mind and he won't stop until he's succeeded. This is why it's imperative to keep Shawnee close and adversely turn the tables on her. She doesn't suspect that I'm on to her. I'm hoping she slips up, revealing exactly what her father is up to."

"Yeah, I understand why you'd want to take advantage of her seemingly friendship with Penny. It certainly explains why Penny introduced me as a distant family relative. I'm assuming you told her not to tell Shawnee that I was your brother. "

"Yes, Penny knows you're my brother, but I asked her not mention it to anyone until everything was legally straightened out with the inheritance. When I get ready to spring that news on McDaniel, I want to have all our ducks lined up. This brings me to the other reason I wanted to talk to you. I need to know how things went today."

"Donavan was everything you said he'd be. He's sharp and very cautious which is good considering dad trusted him. I'm scheduled to appear with him in court this Friday. He's going to look over all of my documents and if need be, I told him we're willing to have dad's body raised for DNA testing."

"Jesus, Jacc do you think that's really necessary?"

"I know it's a bit drastic but what choice do we have? Donavan seems to have some doubt I'm legit and who could blame him? You know how many crackpots would love to stake claim to being Charles Ford's heir? You yourself said some guy tried to exhort money from you and dad. I say to be on the safe side, we should cover all of our bases and allow the DNA testing. That way Donavan has concrete evidence to present in court. Even when all my documents check out, it wouldn't hurt to have extra backing. Know what I mean?"

"Yeah, I know you're right. As much as I dislike the idea of having dad's body raised, it may be the only way we can get the proof that will nail this thing to the wall. Was there anything else Donavan mentioned?"

"That was basically it. I told him he could either contact you or me if he needed any additional information or if he decides he needs the DNA samples."

"All right. I'll let you know if I hear from him before you do. The sooner things are taken care of the better. I'm not sure how long I can pacify the other shareholders.

We've got to present a strong front to them sooner or later, preferably sooner. It's late. Sorry if I woke you up. I just needed to let you know what was going on and find out what happened today. I couldn't wait for this evening to be over so I could get a chance to speak with you."

"It's okay, David. I was having trouble falling asleep anyway. Glad we had a chance to talk. As you say it's late. We'll talk some more over breakfast."

"All right Jacc, I'll see you then. Goodnight." Getting up, David quietly left the room. There was certainly a lot to think about, but I was suddenly feeling beat. We'd have plenty of time to discuss things later that day. Getting up, I walked back to bed, climbed in and went to sleep.

Sitting in traffic, I was on my way to the court hearing. Friday had snuck up like a thief in the night. Today was the day that all would be decided. David and I had waited patiently to hear back from Donavan. As it turned out, I received a call from him two days later stating that all my documents had checked out, but as a precautionary, he wanted to go ahead with the DNA testing. He also stated that it wouldn't be necessary to exhume dad's body because tissue specimens from his autopsy could be used. This was a relief to both David and I. Neither one of us wanted to go to those measures, but would have if it had been required. After talking with Donavan, I paid a visit to one of the DNA centers he recommended to have my sample collected.

Driving into the downtown-parking garage, I parked the car and got out. The probate court was located in the Richard J. Daley Center. Entering the building, I was immediately stopped by security and asked to empty my pockets. I placed my wallet and keys on the moving surveillance belt. Once scanned, I picked up my articles and headed to the elevators. Stepping out of the elevator on the floor where the court proceeding was about to begin, I walked up to Donavan and shook his hand.

"Mr. Donavan, it's good to see you."

"Thank you, Jacc. Shall we head inside? I'm sure you're ready to get this over with."

"You bet I am. Let's go." Donavan pulled opened the door to the courtroom and we walked in. Besides the judge, the court stenographer, and the bailiff, the courtroom was empty.

Sitting high up on his bench, the judge watched as we approached him. "Counsel, I understand there's been new developments since the last court appearance."

"That's correct, Your Honor. I'm asking the court to vacate the motion to have Jaccson Ford declared dead."

"On what grounds are you making this request, Counsel?"

"Your Honor, I'm asking on the grounds that Mr. Jaccson Ford has contacted his biological brother, Mr. David Ford and is in fact alive."

"And is Mr. Jaccson Ford present now?"

"Yes, Your Honor, he is." The judge peered over his wire frame glasses at me. "Are you Mr. Jaccson Ford, son of the late Charles H. Ford?"

"Yes, Your Honor, I am."

"Mr. Ford, you were well on your way to being declared legally dead. Can you tell the court where you've been all this time and why you decided to come forward now?"

"Yes, Your Honor, I can. My relationship with my father was a very strained one. Thirteen years ago we had a major disagreement. Because of it, I distanced myself from my father as well as cut all ties with my family. In retrospect, I realize it was foolish and I regret it tremendously. I'd actually been contemplating contacting my family for some time, but I was afraid of their rejection after so long of a time lapse. It was only recently that I learned of my father's death through the obituary column of an old newspaper. Knowing that I couldn't put things off any longer, I decided to come home."

"Counsel, do you have admissible evidence that supports Mr. Ford's claims and verifies his identity?"

"Yes, Your Honor, I do. I'm prepared to submit all the required documents needed to verify Mr. Ford's identity along with DNA test results that verifies the deceased paternity." Donavan handed the bailiff his documentation who in turn handed it to the judge. Opening up the folder, the judge skimmed through its contents before he glanced up.

"We'll recess until one o'clock. This will give me time to carefully look over these documents and render a final decision. Court is in recess." Rising up, the judge turned and left the courtroom as Donavan and I headed out into the main lobby. "That was a very impressive speech you gave, Jacc."

"Impressive, but true, let's just hope the judge is impressed enough to rule in my favor."

"Are you kidding? This is an airtight case. The DNA tests prove without a shadow of a doubt that Charles Ford is your father."

"Well, we have some time to kill. I'm going to grab a bite to eat. Care to join me?"

"Actually, I'm going to stop by my office. I'll meet you back here at one."

"All right, I'll see you later."

Stepping onto the elevator, we rode down to the main lobby and exited the building. Going our separate ways, I walked a few blocks until I came to a quaint Italian restaurant. Pulling open the door, I walked in and waited for the matradee to seat me.

Once seated, I quickly glanced over the menu and placed my order. As I waited for my food, my cell phone rang. "Hello, Jacc speaking."

"*Hi, Jacc, it's David.*"

THE HOUSE THAT JACC BUILT

"David, what's going on?"

"*How much longer do you think you're going to be?*"

"Actually, I'm at lunch right now. The judge hasn't made a ruling yet. He took a recess so he could evaluate everything. Why, what's going on? Has something happened?"

"*Yeah, you bet it has. The shareholders are calling for an emergency meeting this afternoon. It seems like someone's been stirring the pot. There's talk about a takeover drawing near and they're ready to sell. I'll bet my life on it, McDaniel is trying to make them an offer they can't refuse. I don't know if I can hold them off. We really need this thing with the inheritance to be a done deal. I need you at the meeting.*"

"The court hearing resumes at one. I'll call you when it's all over then I'll head down there. I got a feeling things are going to go as we want as far as the court proceeding. Do your best to hold things together until I arrive. The shareholders aren't going to know what hit them."

"*All right, I'll do what I can on this end. Talk to you soon.*"

Hanging up, I began eating the food that had been placed in front of me. The sooner the judge made his decision the better. This day was turning out to be climatic on all fronts.

"After careful review of all the documents that were presented, I've concluded that you are in fact Charles H. Ford's eldest son, Jaccson Ford. Therefore, as one of the legal heirs to the Ford Estate, I'm granting the petition that the assets your father left you in his will be awarded to you effective immediately." My face lit up in a smile as I tuned to Donavan and patted him on the back. "All right, this is fantastic!"

"Yes, it is," he said as his own face lit up in a smile. I turned back to the judge. "Your Honor, I want to thank you."

"The best of luck to you. Court is now adjourned." Rising up, the judge left the courtroom and headed to his chambers. "Jacc, I'll get started on the necessary paperwork to have everything turned over to you."

"Thanks, you can reach me at the office if something comes up. I'm heading there now. David says something major has cropped up. This news couldn't have come at a better time."

"Definitely, I know you and David are going to give them hell. I'll talk with you later."

Leaving the courtroom, I hurried out of the building. I called David as I walked to the parking garage. Finally reaching the parking garage, I slid behind the wheel once I collected the car. As I maneuvered my way in and out of traffic, I thought about all that had transpired.

Gaining my inheritance was just the preliminary. The real battle was officially underway. It was time for the technical knockout.

STAND TALL

For Those Who Continue to Rise

When is it time to give up?
When do I say enough is enough?
I've often asked this question?
Perhaps when I start to drown in depression?
Because I've lost everything and have nothing to show for myself
Am I supposed to stop trying?
Hang my head and start crying?
Maybe I should crawl into a corner and pray to be put on a shelf?
No, I say I should never give up
Even when I feel enough is enough
I should stand tall
After a fall
Even when I want to bawl
Because as I recall
It takes away the shame of it all

–Diane –

*C*hapter Ten ✍

"**GOOD** afternoon, thank you for attending this emergency shareholders' meeting. I'm David Ford, Chairman and CEO of Charles Ford Builders. I'd like to call the board meeting to order. As I introduce the rest of the board members, I ask that each member stand to be recognized. First we have Michael D. Tavis, chairman and CEO of Tavis Enterprises, one of the largest oil companies in the US. Next, we have Paul Edwards, chairman and CEO of Edwards Garden Inn. Next to him we have Darlene Knowles, Chairman and CEO of Dream Look Cosmetics. Then there's Carol Payne, President and chairman of Payne, O'Connor, and Associates. Next there's Jeffrey Hollister, Chairman and CEO of Hollister Dynamics. Then there's Oliver Forester, President and Chairman of Forester Internationals. Next there's Ronald Johnson, Chairman and CEO of Aero Crafts Solutions, Next is Kyle Hillman, CEO and Chairman of Pacific Motors. Now that everyone has been introduced, I'll turn it over to Kyle Hamilton who will explain why this special meeting has been called."

Just as Hamilton stood up, I opened the door to the boardroom and strolled in. By the look on everyone's face, I was an unexpected intrusion and definitely didn't belong there. David was the only one in the room who was glad to see me for obvious reasons. I noticed the smug look on his face. It was as if he were thinking; *this is going to be good. Let him have it, Jacc.* I let my eyes travel around the room taking in all the key players. Never in a million years would any of them have guessed the man standing in front of them was once a homeless man living on the streets of Chicago. To make matters worse, a once homeless man now held the controlling shares in the corporate empire they each had a stake in. I noticed Hamilton especially looked annoyed that he'd been interrupted. "Can we help you? If you're lost then I suggest you find out where you're supposed to be because we're in the middle of a very important meeting."

Not in the least bit intimidated, I smirked. "Actually, I'm exactly where I'm supposed to be. Ladies and gentlemen, allow me to introduce myself. I'm Jaccson Ford, Charles Ford's eldest son, David's older brother, and the shareholder with controlling shares in this company. So, you see, Hamilton, I'm actually were I need to be since this is an emergency meeting to discuss the future of the company and avoid a possible takeover."

Shock and gasps could be heard throughout the room as chaos ran ramped. "What the hell is the meaning of this?" Jeffrey Hollister stood up. "This is an outrage," Paul Edwards joined him. "Outrage doesn't even describe this, Hamilton added. "Stupidity would be more appropriate. David, you can't possibly think we'd be foolish enough to believe this imposter is Charles Ford's oldest son? It's obvious this is a cheap desperate attempt on your part to try to maintain control of your father's company."

"David, I don't understand," Carol Payne looked utterly confused. "Isn't this the man you recently brought on board as a consultant? Richard Smith, I believe you said was his name?"

Taking delight in everyone's upset, David let his eyes canvass the entire room before they finally rested on Ms. Payne. "That's right, Carol. I did introduce him as Richard Smith, an independent consultant. However, he's really my biological brother. I brought Jacc on board as Mr. Smith to get the lay of the land without having to deal with a whole lot of unwanted questions not to mention suspicions while we hammered out the legal matter concerning our father's estate."

David turned to Hamilton. "Kyle, he's not an imposter."

Deciding to lend David some support, I walked to the front of the room.

"If everyone will settle down, everything will be explained to you. I know this news is confusing if not upsetting for some of you, but the fact remains I am Charles Ford's eldest son. All the legal proceedings have taken place. Mandated by the probate court, my inheritance, which includes the controlling shares of the company, are to be immediately transferred over to me. I can assure you David didn't hire me to pretend to be his brother or Charles Ford's heir. In fact, to ease all your doubts and fears, we'll settle this once and for all by having a conference call to Mr. Stan Donovan, my father's attorney and longtime friend."

Picking up the phone, I dialed Donavan's office.

"Thank you for calling Donavan and Brown's law firm. How can I direct your call?"

"I'd like to speak with Mr. Donavan."

"Your name, sir?"

"Jaccson Ford."

"One moment, Mr. Ford, I'll transfer you." I glanced around the room while I waited. The tension was strong and emotions were high as everyone waited.

"Hello, Jacc, I thought you'd be out celebrating after today's events. What can I do for you?"

"Uh, well, the celebrating will come later. Right now I'm in the middle of an emergency board meeting.

"Geez, they didn't waste any time, did they?"

"No, they didn't. Listen, Stan, I know this is short notice, but I'd like to put you on speakerphone and confirm to the rest of the board exactly what my relationship is with the company. There seems to be doubt about my identity and to clear up the matter, I feel it would be best coming from the legal executor of my father's Estate."

"Sure, if it will help smooth things out, why not?"

"Thanks, Stan." I pressed the button on the phone console. "Go ahead, Stan."

"Good Afternoon, members of the board, this is Stan Donavan. As many of you know, I'm the legal executor of the Charles Ford Estate. With great pleasure, I'd like to say the gentleman standing before you is very much Charles Ford's

oldest son. Earlier today, I was in attendance with the gentleman at a probate hearing to petition the release of all assets that were willed to him by his late father. After carefully reviewing all the submitted documents, which included DNA testing, presiding Judge, Michael Richardson, mandated the assets be turned over to the gentleman standing before you. As all of you are aware, Charles Ford left the bulk of his shares to his oldest son, which in a court of law, has been proven to be alive and well. Ladies and Gentlemen of the board, I present to you, Jaccson Ford."

Silent outrage glinted in several of the board member's eyes as the reality of what Donavan had just told them sunk in. It was obvious to me that several of the members, and especially Hamilton, probably were the ones that would have gained the most from selling their shares to McDaniel.

"Thanks Stan," I said as I quickly glanced at David. The smugness on his face was definitely the sign of victory.

"You're welcome, Jacc. I'll have all the necessary paperwork sent over to you by messenger this afternoon. Was there anything else I can assist you with?"

"Actually, there is, but it has to do with a whole different and private matter."

"I see. Stop by my office any time and we'll talk. Ladies and Gentlemen, I'll be making my departure, and Jacc?"

"Yes."

"Congratulations, son, your father would be proud of you."

"Thank you."

"You're welcome. Bye."

Disconnecting the speakerphone, I turned to the person taking the minutes. "Did you get everything down?"

"Yes, I did."

"Excellent. Now that everyone knows where I stand. I say we get down to the business at hand. First off, let me assure you, that the future looks very bright for Charles Ford Builders. I know there has been some concern about the future of the company and the direction in which it is headed. As I'm sure you're aware McDaniel has put a bid on the table for the company. I know many of you if not all were prepared to vote on the buyout, but seeing that I own over fifty percent of the shares along with David's shares, McDaniel still won't be victorious in a takeover. If they were to buy out all of your shares, it still won't be enough."

Hamilton turned to David. "Of all the lowdown stunts, this is how you're going to play this? You deliberately deceived us into thinking your brother was someone else so you could buy sometime to pull this whole thing off!"

"Besides, McDaniel, you must be the one that's going to gain the most from the takeover. Tell me, what type of perks did he throw in as well? Anyone in my position would have done the same thing. This company was my father's life and he would have wanted it to stay within the family. Don't make this personal, Hamilton. It's just business. Everything has been done above board and legally. All in favor of casting a vote on accepting a buyout bid please signify by a showing of your hand."

With the exception of Hamilton, no one else in the room raised their hand. It was clear that everyone had rethought their position. Angry, Hamilton got up and stormed out of the meeting.

David turned his attention back to the other board members. "I want to thank you for your continued faith and belief in Charles Ford Builders. Let me assure you the company is building a stronger, better, platform, which will continue to bring in profits. We believe in our products and our commitment to providing exemplary service is what has and will continue to separate us from our competitors. Are there any other issues on the agenda that need to be addressed?" When no one raised any concerns, David ended the meeting. "Minutes of the meeting will be distributed for your approval as you leave. The meeting is now adjourned." Everyone got up and began leaving the boardroom. It was obvious they were still wheeling from these new turns of events. I'm sure Hamilton couldn't wait to let McDaniel know exactly what went down. For the remaining of the afternoon, David consulted with the company's public relations department about doing a press conference to announce my return. I wasn't sure if I was ready for the media attention that was bound to come with the announcement, especially since I hadn't had a chance to even tell Diane. I decided to tell him over dinner that night. We were scheduled to meet Penny and a few of David's friends at a restaurant in celebration of regaining control of the company. Hopefully, I'll get a chance to talk with David alone sometime during the evening.

"To the Ford brothers and their father's legacy, may your future be as bright as the stars shinning above."

The interior design of the posh downtown Italian restaurant was exquisite. It was one of Penny's favorite restaurants. It was also where David had proposed to her. She was dressed beautifully in an elegant shimmering black evening dress. David and I were also dressed for the occasion. Wearing our finest dark suits, we epitomized class and style. Two of his business associates had joined us along with their wives. I was glad David and Penny hadn't invited Shawnee. I didn't want to have to endure another wretched evening spent in her company. Besides, I didn't mind being the odd man out.

Jessica Tolliver, wife of David's closest friend Jeremy Tolliver, turned to me. "Tell me, Jacc, are you a golfer?"

"I'm afraid not. I never took the time to learn the game."

"You're kidding?" Jeremy said. Shock was apparent in his eyes as he regarded me with newfound curiosity.

"You mean to tell me that Charles Ford actually has a son that's not the next Payne Stewart protégée? Golf was definitely your dad's game. In fact, its David's game as well. I'd thought you'd have acquired both your father's and brother's love of the sport."

"Jeremy, you'll soon learn I march to the beat of a different drummer. I've never been one to fall in line with family tradition. If golf's David's thing, I'm glad for him, but I definitely don't want to be molded into a Payne Stewart protégée. Mr. Stewart was an excellent golfer and even years after his passing, I'm sure he's missed by his adoring fans, but I must say I never liked the guy's sporting attire. Give me a break, can a guy wearing knickers on the golf course be taken seriously?"

"Sure he can," Eric Woodard, David's other friend interjected. "Just ask David, he has a pair he wears all the time!" It was my turn to look shocked as I glanced at my brother. All of the sudden everyone burst out laughing. The mere thought of David wearing those ridiculous knickers, which exposed his bony legs was unimaginable if not truly laughable. My laugher was cut short when I noticed the waiter seating her and another gentleman at a nearby table.

Looking around, she noticed our table. Getting up, she headed toward us. Dressed in a sleek form fitting black dress, Shawnee reminded me of a poisonous snake as she slithered her way up to our table. "What do we have here? Looks like a celebration no doubt."

Penny smiled. "Shawnee, how are you? I had no idea you were dinning here tonight."

"Save it, Penny. There's no need for us to pretend anymore. As far as I'm concerned the kid gloves are off. I was at my father's office earlier and I had the unfortunate pleasure of witnessing Kyle Hamilton practically break down in tears in my father's office. Apparently their deal fell through and it's all because of this return from the dead jerk!"

Her eyes raged with anger as she turned and faced me. "You may or may not be Charles Ford's son, but you'll never fit in here. I knew you were nothing but worthless scum the moment I laid eyes on. Why did you have to come back and mess everything up? Go back to the gutter where you belong!"

"Shawnee, that's enough!" David stood up. "This kind of behavior is outrageous. This isn't the time or place to discuss the matter."

"Shut up, David. You were the mastermind behind this whole scam. That's what this is, you know? I don't believe for one minute this guy is your brother. Where did you find him, in a circus, of better yet, you probably just picked him up right off the street!" Penny stood up.

"Shawnee, I think you'd better leave or I might not be responsible for my actions."

"Ha! Is that a threat?"

"Is everything all right?" In the mist of all the commotion, no one noticed that Shawnee's date had strolled over to our table. "Shawnee, are you all right? Are these people giving you any trouble?"

Fed up, I stood. "Look, pal, the only trouble in this place is the woman you had the misfortune to walk in here with. If you really want to avoid any real trouble, I suggest you either go back to your own table or leave all altogether."

"It's, okay, Tom, let's just leave. I've suddenly lost my appetite. It seems that the caliber of people they let in here has gone down." She glanced at me on more time before she turned and walked out with her date. "You may have won this round, but you can bet your last dollar, I'm going to win the war. I will find a way to prove you are a fraud even if I have to spend a lifetime doing it."

"Wow, talk about swallowing a bitter pill, I'd say she swallowed the whole damn bottle."

"It just goes to show you who your real friends are. I don't know about anyone else, but after that scene I could really use a drink. Would anyone care to join me in the bar?" Penny looked around. Jeremy and his wife along with Eric and his wife all stood up. I remained sitting.

"David, are you and Jacc coming?"

"Actually, Penny, I wanted to speak with David for a minute alone. We'll join you in a little while."

"All right then, see you guys in a bit." They all headed toward the bar. Sitting back in his seat, David looked at me. "So, what gives? Don't tell me you're worried about Shawnee's threats. She and her dad might as well get over it. There isn't a darn thing they can do to reverse today's outcome on all fronts. It's a done deal."

"I'm not particularly worried about Shawnee or her father, but I am concerned about your plans to have a full scale press conference. David, do you mind if we hold off on it just a little while?"

"I'm afraid I can't hold off on the press conference. We owe it to all our employees as well as our investors to know that there's a new head of the company. In fact, the conference has been scheduled for tomorrow afternoon. Jacc, don't tell me you're camera shy?"

I wasn't in the least bit shy, but if it would prevent David from announcing on national TV my true identity then I'd gladly develop a sudden case of shyness. Not wanting to the risk my identity being discovered before I was able to bring Diane back safely with me, I decided to go along with David's assumption. "Yeah, I don't feel comfortable about a press conference. If there has to be an announcement, why not just do some type of statement or press release? I just really would prefer not to have my face plastered all over the TV. Can you imagine the attention it would bring? We wouldn't have any peace. I say we handle this as low key as possible."

Despite David's sigh, I knew I had him. "All right, Jacc, we'll play it your way. If it's low key you want, then its low key you'll get. I'll let the media relations department know about the change tomorrow. We'll have to give them some reason why you've decided to squash the conference. We can simply say you were feeling under the weather; therefore you weren't able to attend a live conference."

"Sounds good to me, in fact, it's perfect. Now that we've straightened that out, I say we go find the rest of our party."

"I'm with you on that." Getting up, we headed to the bar and joined the others.

As I lay awake, I turned over and punched my pillow before I let my head fall back on it. Nothing spectacular was going on. I was just having another sleepless night staring off into space. For the past hour or so, I was consumed with thoughts of Diane. Feeling especially lonely, I missed her something fierce. The time was drawing very near when all was going to be right in our world. One of the first things I was going to do when I finally brought her home is buy her an engagement ring. Okay, so I'm jumping the gun by assuming she's going to accept my marriage proposal, but I just can't help it. I love Diane and I know she loves me. She's the woman I want to see first thing in the morning, the woman I want to grow old with, she's the woman I want to be the mother of my children. Had anyone asked me years ago if I'd ever see myself as a married man with a family, I'd have told them flat out no. All that had changed since I met Diane. Being homeless, you're in constant survival mold. Rarely do you have time to plan beyond one day to the next least of all plan on sharing your life with another human being. I've often heard many homeless people say that trying to have a real relationship with anyone who's in the same boat as your self is just plain crazy.

Normally I would be inclined to agree with them, but that was before I met Daryl. His fortitude and sheer determination to hold it all together for the sake of love was admiral. Given the right opportunity, I know Daryl would be there a 110 percent for Clarice and her children. Despite all the pessimistic views I'd heard from the homeless about love, I still believed in it. No matter how many countless reasons the homeless give to discourage each other from extending themselves, the one that's at the forefront is two homeless people can't help each other because neither one of them has anything to offer.

What people don't realize is its love that's keeps me up late making plans for the future with the most wonderful woman I've ever met. Its love that motivates me to strive to build a future for us in the mist of our shattered downtrodden lives. Its love that makes me want to go the extra mile when by all logic, I should have thrown in the towel and given up a long time ago. It's love that has kept her by my side even when she knew I had nothing to offer. It's love that will keep her by my side even if I have millions one day and lose it the next. It's love for God's people that's going to allow me to bless them even if they wouldn't give so freely of themselves. Who can understand the mystery of love? All we really know is it allows us to look beyond an individual's shortcoming and really understand their needs. We know it's a healer of the mind, body, and soul. To go through life claiming that you don't deserve or need love just because you're poor or homeless makes no sense. The ability to give and receive love shouldn't be equated on how successful you are.

Throughout my life, I've learned true wealth comes from within. A person can be rich in faith, love, joy, understanding, and courage. Each of us has a part to play in this human experience we call life. We should be constantly learning and growing. What I've learned recently is not to allow hurt feelings keep you away from those you love. As Papa Joe says, we're all on borrowed time and we don't get a dress rehearsal in life.

As I lay here in bed, that familiar urgency suddenly washed over me. I have one shot at getting this thing right within my soul and with God. When I started on this journey, I had no idea about the blessing God had stored up for me.

Nor had I anticipated complete forgiveness from David. Thank God we've gotten past our own pain to bridge the thirteen-year gap. The more I thought about it, the more I began to wonder about Diane's rift with her own family. Knowing all too well how hard it is to reconnect with them after you'd been so distant, I wondered if Diane ever felt bad or regretted not at least making more of a attempt to stay connected.

Thinking back, I recalled our first conversation. She didn't go into great detail about what was going on with her family, but I do remember she did mention something about an aunt who surprisingly sounded very much like my dad. Was Diane also pressured into living a life that she didn't necessarily want? Why is it, as a child, you're often molded to be someone that may not necessarily be who you are? Child development is so important. Everyone should be allowed to develop their own personality. It'll lead them to setting goals that are conducive to who they really are. God knows I'd gone through that enough myself. If and when I become a parent, I'm certainly going to allow my children freedom to express themselves and discover exactly who they are for themselves.

This was a quality that my mom had. No matter what, she was supportive of my efforts. She truly understood my need to find my own way. Now that I think about it, I hadn't had any recent nightmares or dreams about my parents. I noticed that several days ago. It was almost as if my mind and soul were truly at peace. It was a peace and comfort I hadn't experienced in a long time. Dwelling inside a home, and not having to figure out where I could take a shower or not having to stand in line for hours just to eat certainly had removed a heavy weight off of my shoulders. The amenities that were once absent from my life were now laid at my feet. It was as if I were suddenly thrown into paradise. The simple things such as watching TV, sleeping late, and being able to eat what I wanted when I wanted it were now privileges I looked forward to with great joy and anticipation. I was like a kid who had been let loose inside toy store. Talk about a culture shock, I felt like I'd finally arrived home after living in another world for the past year. The whole time I was on the trail, I felt like I was on some kind of never ending journey only now the journey had finally ended and I could really relax.

The best part about adjusting to having a place to live was I didn't have to worry about where I was going to sleep at night. This alone was enough to motivate anyone to seek housing. Closing my eyes, I finally let the heaviness of my body relax as I eventually drifted off to sleep. My last waking thought was that of Diane as I wished her sweet dreams.

"What's the matter, Diane? You can't sleep?"
"Actually, Hattie, I was dreaming about Jacc when

something woke me up. God, I hope he's okay. I rarely remember my dreams, but this one was strange. I was walking through a field of lilies as I waited for Jacc. I stopped and turned around when I heard him call my name. He started running toward me only he never reached me. Although he was actually running, the distance between us wasn't closing in. It was as if he weren't moving at all, yet he was definitely running toward me. Hattie, it was the weirdest thing I ever saw. Not sure if he saw me, I called out to him and waited to see if he'd finally catch up with me. Tired of waiting, I began to run toward him and the most bizarre thing happened. As I ran to him, the distance between us finally started closing and then I literally ran right through him. Hattie, I ran right through Jacc as if he were transparent. Freaking out, I turned around and there he was still running. As I continued to watch him run I saw him run right into my arms only it wasn't me because I was standing far away. There was Jacc standing there holding me and it wasn't me. That's when I woke up. That dream scared the living daylights out me. Hattie, what do you suppose it all means?

"It's hard to say, Diane. That was some dream. Could be that you and Jacc might have had some type of disagreement and that's why you didn't connect, why he didn't catch you and why you ran right through him. Then again, it kinda sounds like he was a ghost."

"Or I was one. The whole thing was just too weird. I hope he's all right. I miss him and I just want him to return safely. This waiting around twiddling my thumbs is driving me crazy. I shouldn't have let him leave."

"And just how were you gonna stop him, Diane? Short of tying the man up to keep him from leaving, how were you gonna prevent it? I know you miss him, and if I were you when he did show his face around here again, I'd give him a piece of my mind, but the truth is you couldn't have stopped him from going if you tried. Jacc had it in his mind to leave for whatever reasons and there was nothing any of us could have done to stop him. Darn shame, you have to wonder what the heck is going on. I know the waiting is killing you, but you got no choice but to wait this out. I really couldn't tell you what your dream meant. Sometimes the mind subconsciously shows us things that may or may not mean anything. Come on, it's late and we need to get some sleep. Jacc will be back soon enough. Maybe you can ask him what your dream meant."

"Jacc, are you sure this is what you want to do? At least think about it. And for Pete's sake, talk this over with David." I was sitting in Donavan's office. I'd stopped by to discuss transferring some of my stock over to David so he would have controlling interest in the business. I'd just gone over everything in great detail about what I wanted to do and I also made up my will and gave Donavan a copy of it. He obviously thought I was making a grave mistake. He didn't understand why I'd want to step down and give David controlling interest in the company. Sighing, I stood up and walked over to the window. The panoramic view of the bustling city below could be seen high up on the twentieth floor of the office complex. Turning around, I looked at Donavan. It was obvious why my father trusted the man. He also had a no nonsense approach to business and was as shrewd as they came. A man who also thirsts for power, it was clear he didn't suffer fouls easily, and a fool he thought I was, especially since I didn't have to earn the power that had been given to me. I should be so lucky to have inherited it.

"Donavan—"

"Jacc, you know we're way past formalities. Just call me Stan."

"All right, Stan, I know you think I'm being foolish, but I've made up my mind. Let me explain something. I'm not sure how much you know about my relationship with my father. Dad had this vision of me stepping into his shoes and I had a totally different vision which had nothing to do with the family business. Now given the fact that I was young and perhaps impetuous, it stands to reason I didn't have a grasp of what I wanted out of life. Well, that maybe true, but I also knew what I didn't want. Dad shouldn't have left me with controlling interest. David is more qualified to fill his shoes. CFB is his life. Just like dad, he has put his heart and soul into the business."

"Jacc, I've known your father for a long time and I can assure you Charles never did anything on a fluke. He must have had his reason for doing what he did. You know it's not the worst thing in the world for a man to have inherited a fortune. Thank God, you came to your damn senses and decided to return home when you did."

"That's just it, Stan. I came home for an entirely different reason than the inheritance or to head up CFB. I came home because I'd learned my father had died and to ask my brother for a business loan. It's not that I'm ungrateful for the inheritance; it's just that it was totally unexpected and I'm not really sure why dad did it. Somehow, I can't help feel like David got cheated. This is why I want to have some of my stocks transferred over to him. I want to transfer enough of my shares to him so he'll have the actual numbers to be the big cheese and not I. Call it a reversing of numbers, if you will. David can have the amount of shares that I currently have and I'll be left with the amount of shares he has. That way he can take his rightful place in the company and I can be free to do what I need to do for myself."

"Jacc, what I don't understand is why you just didn't have the stock transferred over to David in the beginning since you never had any real intention of taking over Charles Ford Builders?"

"For starters, everything was thrown at me from the moment I arrived home. Then there was the whole issue with proving my identity and given the time constraints of the possible takeover, it just seemed safer and faster to allow everything to play out in court the way it did. I didn't want to take the risk of slowing things up. I knew that once it was proven I was really Jaccson Ford, then all the assets would be released immediately. Given that the shareholders called for the emergency meeting, it was a good thing that I played it that way. Once everything was taken care of, I knew I would simply have whatever amount of shares transferred over to David which would make him the new corporate head."

"I see. It's a good thing you had David postpone the press release. If this is really what you want, then I have no choice but to honor your wishes. I'll go ahead and have the paperwork started. I'll need the number of shares you want to transfer and the stock certificates. As far as your will, I'll go ahead and take care of that as well. Was there anything else you needed to have taken care of?"

I walked over to Donavan's desk and extended my hand. "No, that's about it, Stan. I want to thank you for all your help." Gripping my hand in a firm handshake, he smiled. "No problem, Jacc. If you ever need any legal help or advice, just let me know."

"I will, and thanks again." Turning around, I walked out of his office. Glad that was taken care of, I decided to go for a drive to clear my head. As far as I was concerned, it was time for me to start preparing for the next phase in my life.

I drove around several times before I finally found a parking space. Brookfield Zoo, as always, was crowded. It was one my mother's favorite places to visit. Mom was an animal lover. She often brought David and I to the zoo when we were children. Somehow driving to the zoo was therapeutic for me. It was where I often felt closest to mom. Getting out of the car, I walked to the admissions desk and paid the fee before entering the zoo. Several groups of children, obviously on a field trip, clamored about in a chaotic cluster.

It was the middle of the afternoon and the zoo was filled with lots of people. Mothers pushed baby strollers, while dads hoisted toddlers on their shoulders and strolled through the grounds. Children laughed, and tourists took snapshots of all kinds of animals. I strolled by several zoo attractions and peered in at the animals like the many spectators who had come to get a look at God's magnificent creatures. There was something about the animals that somehow put everything in perspective. As I studied them, I was reminded of what Diane had once said about life being simple and uncomplicated for them. I've often wondered why humans with all of our wisdom and higher intellect, can't figure out we're all striving for the same thing.

It doesn't matter what race, culture, or country a person originated from, every human being's basic needs are the same. Why does it have to be all about the survival of the fittest? If we're really all living within a Darwin type of module, then the homeless are the one's truly passing the test. They're the one surviving without all of the conveniences that society has and is fighting to maintain. If you were to take away all of our technology and our trinkets, you'll find each of us trying to survive from the very raw instincts we were all born with. You'll also find we can and will adapt to any and every environmental change within our world. Instinctively man realizes that in order to survive, he has to become adaptable.

Realizing I was hungry, I looked around for a place to get a bite to eat. Stopping off at a concession stand, I brought a hot dog and a soda. Looking around for a bench, I found one near a shady tree. "Say mister, can you spare some change?" I was about to take a bite of my hotdog when a man came out of nowhere. Being homeless, you learn to detect who's homeless. The guy had all the telltale signs. He was eyeing my food like he hadn't eaten in days.

"Here." I handed him my hotdog and soda.

"Thanks," he said as he snatched the bun from my hand and sank down on the bench. I've never seen anyone eat so fast. In one gulp, the food was gone and after a swig or two so was the soda. Letting out a loud burp, the guy smiled.

"Thank you, I was starving." Sitting down, I looked at the man. He looked to be around fifty or so and he had that typical disheveled homeless look. I was kind of surprised to see a homeless guy hanging out at the zoo since it was so far out in the suburbs. Then again, why should I be surprised? Being homeless, you tend to find out-of-the-way places to dwell.

"So what's your name?"

"Why, what's it to you?" The guy eyed me suspiciously. He probably thought I was an undercover cop.

"You Five-O?" I laughed. It was just as I suspected.

"No, I'm not a cop. I was just curious is all. I like to know who I'm talking to. My name is Jacc." I stuck out my hand. "Nice to meet you." Hesitating, he stared at my hand a moment before he finally accepted my handshake.

"Nice to meet you too, my name is Lou."

"Lou, how long have you been on the trail?"

"Ha! What do you know about being on the trail? You don't look like you'd be anywhere near a homeless trail!"

I smiled. "Looks can be deceiving, Lou. You'd be surprised what I know about the trail. There was a time not too long ago when I was homeless and sleeping anywhere I could. There are some things in a man's life that he never forgets. You know what I mean?"

"Yeah, I guess I do. So, what happened? You hit the

lottery or something? Man, I wouldn't have put you as being a tramp on the trail?"

"No, I didn't hit the lottery. Let's just say God decided to bestow a blessing on me just like I'm about to do for you."

Reaching in my pocket, I took out my wallet and pulled out a hundred dollar bill. "Here, enjoy it. Maybe you can get yourself a room for the night or something."

His eyes widen in surprise as he snatched the money. Jumping up, his face lit up in a bright smile. "Thanks, Jacc, for the food and everything. Man this is a blessing for real. Thanks again, and take care!" I smiled as I watched him run off. He probably was going back to his camp and brag about his good fortune. Getting up, I decided to head home. As much as I had been avoiding it, it was time I told David about my plans.

WHEN ALL ELSE IS SAID AND DONE

The Calling Of Life

When all else is said and done
When the battle is over and you've finally won
And celebration has just begun
With the setting of the day's sun
Know that you've done your best
As the outcome tells the rest
For tomorrow you'll follow the call
Embarking on new tasks as you give it your all
Because when all else is said and done
You'll know you were the one
That made it possible by bringing hope
To those who're trying to cope
Yet feel their goals are way out of scope
You'll prove victory is yours
As you spread your wings and soar
Reaching for your star
Proving it isn't too far
Yes, you'll be the one
When all else is said and done
You'll do your best
By passing every test
As the outcome tells the rest

—Jacc—

*C*hapter Eleven ✍

"**YOU'RE** leaving, aren't you? Don't bother denying it, Jacc. I've known for several days that you were going to leave." David and I were relaxing in the great room. He was right. I was leaving. Two weeks had gone by and I was scheduled to meet Diane tomorrow at noon. Nothing was going to keep me from going back for her. Not sure when he'd figured out I was planning on leaving, I turned in my chair and stared at him. "I wasn't going to deny anything. You're right, David, I leaving in the morning. I have to go back."

"Why, for heaven's sake? Why do you need to go back? What in God's name are you going back to, the lousy streets? Come on, give me a break! I knew something wasn't right. Your restlessness, everything about your behavior has been a major giveaway. Something's been weighing heavy on your mind ever since you came back. At first I thought it might have been guilt for not being here when dad died. I mean it would make sense that you'd feel guilty for staying away for so long, but later I attributed your moodiness to stress due to the whole inheritance thing. Heck, we've both been under stress, but now that everything's behind us and things are stable within the company, you'd think you'd be smiling at a bright future. Hell, Jacc you own fifty-five percent of the stock, you're filthy rich, good looking, have a beautiful home to live in, drive an expensive car, and you want to give all this up? I don't understand."

This was the one conversation I'd been trying to avoid for some time. Again, David was right. For the past two weeks, I'd been preoccupied with not only the inheritance and blocking a possible corporate takeover; I'd also been counting the days until I returned for Diane. I knew I'd have to tell David that I was going to leave sooner or later; however, it wasn't like I was going away for good. The plan was to bring Diane back here.

There was also the issue about me continuing to stay on with the company. During the crisis with the takeover, I was more than willing to step up to the plate and help out with things, but the truth was I simply wasn't comfortable with the corporate scene. Besides, I had other plans and they were foremost in my mind. I was more determined than ever to put things into motion. My inheritance had definitely put me in the position to move full speed ahead. God had allowed me the opportunity to be a blessing for so many with a viable plan and I was going to do just that. Totally understanding my brother's confusion and bewilderment, I knew I could no longer avoid telling him everything.

"David, I want you to listen as I tell you a story. It's a love story about a man and a woman and a dream they shared. This story will hopefully help you understand why I have to go back. There once was a young man who found himself down on his luck. He'd fallen as low as a man could fall according to you. Being a survivor, the man learned to survive under the most unimaginable distress in an environment where he didn't really belong. In this environment was a beautiful woman who was also a survivor. It was obvious to the man she didn't belong there either, yet they were both there. Eventually they grew closer and fell in love. Together, they overcame a lot of obstacles and pitfalls. As they struggled to survive, they also began to realize not only were there others like themselves, they felt an overwhelming compassion for all who found themselves caught up in their treacherous cycle. They often dreamed of making life better for people who otherwise were deemed unworthy. Although it was a dream, somehow the man knew if he ever got the opportunity to make the dream become a reality, he was going to make a major impact on so many lives. The man's name is Jacc, and the woman's name is Diane."

David stood up and walked over to the window. He stared out of it for a long time before he finally turned around.

"Why didn't you tell me about Diane from the very beginning? For that matter, why didn't you simply bring her with you?"

"I didn't tell you about her because I didn't know how you'd receive her and I didn't bring her back with me because I didn't know what I'd be walking into. I was worried that you might not receive me as well. I didn't want to subject Diane to any discord if you didn't. I certainly didn't know about the inheritance. As far I was concerned, Dad had cut me out of his will completely. If you'll recall, I asked you to float me a loan when I first arrived home. I was looking to use the money to help finance a plan I feel will help the homeless which brings me to the other issue." Getting up, I walked over to a mahogany desk and opened one of its drawers. Taking out two envelops, I closed the drawer and walked over David. "What's this?" He stared at the envelopes as I handed them to him.

"The one addressed to you is all the necessary paperwork that gives you controlling interest in the business. I met with Donavan earlier today. I had him transfer some of my shares to you so you'd have controlling interest. You now own fifty-five percent of the shares. I own twenty percent. Together we own seventy-five percent which definitely keeps the business in the family since the remaining shares divided among the other shareholders is hardly enough to give anyone controlling interest. David, dad should have left you with controlling interest. Running the family business is and always has been your thing. It's never really been mine. I have a different calling. My experience with homelessness hasn't been in vain. It has opened my eyes to what I'm supposed to be doing with my life. The other envelop is for Diane. It's to be given to her in case something ever happens to me. I don't foresee anything happening, but just in case, I want her to be well taken care of. I'm entrusting it to you for safekeeping."

"I'm speechless, Jacc. I never resented the fact that dad gave you controlling interest. I just assumed he was doing what he considered was the natural order of things since you were the eldest. He held out against all hope that you were going to return and you did. It's just too bad he didn't live long enough to see it happen. Although I was also praying you'd return, I have always tried to look at things from a realistic viewpoint. As heartbroken as it was to face that I may have lost my brother for good, I tried to prepare myself for the fact I may never see you again."

I nodded as I thought about our mom. "David, I understand. Thirteen years is a long time to go without knowing if I were dead or live. You've always been the one in the family with the level head. I remember when I learned mom wasn't going to make it; you did your best to try to prepare me for the reality of it all. I didn't want to accept it, but you knew it was the only way to deal with it. When I went into see her, she made me promise not to alienate you and dad. Not only didn't I not keep my promise to her, I never got a chance to make peace with dad. I know I can't change what happened, but I hope I was able to at least help save the business."

"Jacc, I'm sure if mom and dad were both here, they'd be proud of you. Diane must be a very special lady."

"Yes, she is. I've never known a woman quite like her. Diane has an inner strength and determination that defies any rationale of defeat. She's intelligent, compassionate, and very insightful. I met her while staying in a shelter and in spite of the evil that was done to her inside that sickening place, she managed to hold on to her pride and dignity. She shares my dream to be a blessing to the homeless, but doesn't really think it will ever come to pass. I'm going back for her, David. I'm going to bring her back here where we'll be married. I love her and I want nothing but the best for her. Once we get settled in our own home, we'll begin our lives together doing what we were called to do."

"Jacc, I glad you've found someone that makes you happy. I won't stand in your way. You're my brother, and I want the best for you. You're leaving was a result of Dad trying to pressure you to live a life that you didn't want. Everyone is entitled to pursue their own dreams. You have my full support in all your endeavors. I'm behind you all the way."

"Thanks, David, that means a lot to me. I'll leave first thing in the morning. As soon as I've had time to talk to Diane, we'll head back home. It might be best if I don't drive down. I'll take the train there and back."

"All right, just call and I'll have someone pick you up at the train station when you return. Are you going to be alright?"

"Yeah, I'll be fine. I'd just rather avoid any

problems if all possible. Within the homeless population, people get to know you, including the seedy ones."

"Be careful, Jacc. I don't want to lose you again."

Too excited to sleep, I was up early the next morning. Today I would be reunited with Diane. Just as I was about to step into the shower, David opened my bedroom door and stuck his head in. "Morning, Jacc. I'm heading out for a while. I'll be back in an hour to take you to the train station."

"Thanks David, I appreciate it."

"No problem. That's what brothers are for. See you later." I walked into the bathroom and stepped into the shower. My mind was racing a mile a minute as I thought about my conversation with David the previous night. I'm glad we were growing closer. It had been a long time coming. I'm sure our mom would be delighted if she were here. The reunion between David and I had been way overdue. The future was definitely looking bright and all was right in the world. Soon, I'll be with Diane and we'll be heading back home. Who knows, maybe there'll be a double wedding? I envisioned Diane dressed in a beautiful wedding gown and I'd be standing in the crowded great room dressed in a black tuxedo waiting as she gracefully floated down the curved staircase. Talk about being a romantic dreamer, I was on a roll this morning! Turning off the water, I stepped out of the shower, grabbed a towel, and dried off. In an exceptionally good mood, I began to whistle as I quickly pulled on a pair of jeans and donned a pullover sweatshirt. Placing my cell phone and wallet in my pocket, I sat on the bed to put on my socks and shoes. Standing up, I took one last look in the mirror before I headed out the door and downstairs to the kitchen. Hungry as a bear, I couldn't wait to devour the scrumptious breakfast Cook had prepared.

"Say, Keith, what's happening, bro?"

"Oh, Kango, it's you, nothing's happening. What's going on with you?"

"Slow motion, man, you know how it is. Say, where have you been hiding? I haven't seen you or that white stud you were hanging around with in a long time. What, ya'll stop hanging down here in Uptown?

"Kango, I've just been laying low that's all. No big deal."

"Did your partner come down here to the soup kitchen with you today?"

"Why?"

"Oh, I see you don't wanna say if that stud came with you or not. Well, that's too bad because I ran into that broad who's kicking it with him."

"Diane? I don't believe you."

"All the same, it's true. I saw her earlier at the Dollar Store on Wilson Ave. She acted like she didn't have time to talk. She said she was in a hurry to meet up with old boy later today. She wished she could get word to him to just meet her at Sheridan Park. She said it would be easier since she was already in the hood. Believe it or not, I was just passing the message on in case you ran into your friend. Hey, Keith, where are you running off to? Aren't you staying for lunch?"

"Nah, I just remembered something I need to do. Thanks for the information, Kango, I gotta go, bye!"

"Here we are." David drove his car into the train station's parking lot. It's funny how things turn out. I remember my lonely arrival at the station on the day I returned home. Here I was now being driven to the station and seen off like all the other people about to board the waiting train. Unfastening my seat belt, I turned to David and smiled.

"Thanks, again. I'll call you as soon as we are heading home."

"Jacc, are you sure you don't want to drive where you're going? I don't mind taking you back home so you can get your car. Hell, I'll even drive you to the city myself!" Grabbing my jacket off the back seat, I opened the front door and got out. "I'll be fine, David, don't worry. I'll be home before you know it. Tell, you what, why don't you have

Cook prepare a special dinner? I'll be bringing Diane home tonight and that definitely is a celebration."

"Sure, Jacc, whatever you want. Just promise me, you'll be careful and if any type of problem arises, you'll call me immediately."

"David, nothing's going to happen. If it makes you feel better, I will call you if something comes up. See you later." Closing the car door, I followed the crowd as they boarded the train.

Sitting by one of the window seats inside the commuter car, I stared out the window as the train sped down the tracks. Although it had only been two weeks it since I'd last seen Diane, it seemed like it had been forever. Never had a statement rang so true than the one about absent making the heart grow fonder. I missed Diane beyond my comprehension. In fact, if I were truthful, I would also have to admit I missed Keith and the whole gang. They had definitely become my extended family. Once I'd taken care of everything with Diane, I was going to start working on getting everyone else into housing. This year was definitely going to bring about change for everyone. Leaning back in my seat, I closed my eyes. The continuous motion of the train eventually put me to sleep.

"Union Station will be our final stop and destination. We're now approaching Union Station, Downtown Chicago."

One hour later, I woke up just as the conductor was making his announcement. Impatient for my journey to finally be over, I immediately gathered in the aisle with the rest of the passengers when the commuter train came to a screeching halt. The excitement I felt was one I hadn't felt in a long time. I couldn't wait to tell Diane all about my family and the inheritance my father had left. I knew it was going to be hard for her to believe at first, but once I was able to successfully convince her that all her dreams were about to come true in a drastic way, I knew she'd be overwhelmed with unspeakable joy. Soon we were going to be living the life we were meant live. We were also going to bless the homeless by providing what I knew in my heart was a way for them to rise above their current circumstances and finally become homeowners. It was the only righteous and humane thing to do. It's what I believed God wanted.

Union Station was busy with the hustle and bustle of its daily travelers as I stood in the corridor and tried to get my bearings. My eyes quickly scanned the room, searching for the exit. I spotted a clock hanging on a wall near a door that led out to the main street. Realizing I had less than an hour before I was scheduled to meet Diane, I quickened my steps as I made my way through the crowded hall. If I hurried, I'd be able to catch my bus and arrive just in time to meet her at the park. It was fifteen after eleven.

"Hey, Jacc, over here!" Bewildered by who was calling me, I immediately stopped and turned around, searching the crowd as my eyes scanned the room.

"Jacc, right here! Over here, man!" Finally recognizing the voice, I spotted Keith standing a few feet away. I rushed up and gave him a brotherly hug. "What the heck are you doing down here? God, it's good to see you!" Pulling out of the embrace, I searched his face. It suddenly dawned on me something was wrong. Why else would he have come down to meet me? An uneasy feeling suddenly washed over me. There was something unsettling about this reunion. Something definitely wasn't right.

"Keith, what's going on? Is it Diane? Has something happened to her?" My eyes were wide and anxious. Shaking his head, Keith offered a reassuring smile. "Relax. Nothing's happened. Everything's fine. Diane's waiting for you at Sheridan Park in Uptown. That's what I came to tell you. I wanted to let you know the meeting place had been changed. Thank God I caught you before you headed to the other park."

Relieved that Diane was okay, I wondered what had prompted the sudden change in plans. "Thanks for letting me know, Keith. Did she say why she decided to meet at Sheridan Park instead of where we'd originally planned?"

"No, I didn't actually speak with Diane. I ran into Kango earlier. He told me he'd just seen her at the Dollar Store in Uptown. Said she was acting like she was really in a hurry and didn't have time to talk to him. She mentioned she was planning on hooking up with you, but wasn't going to make it in time. Said she wished she could get word for you to meet her at Sheridan Park since she was already in Uptown. He told me all of this when I ran into him a little while later at the soup kitchen. That's when I decided to track you down. So, here I am."

Something in my gut told me things weren't quite right with the whole arrangement. Although I trusted Keith and knew he wouldn't steer me wrong, I felt an uneasy feeling in the pit of my stomach. "Keith, are you sure? Do you really think Kango is a reliable source? The whole thing sounds kind of fishy."

"Yeah, I was thinking the same thing when I saw him, but I didn't want to take a chance of you and Diane missing each other. She's been counting down the days until your return. Been really uptight that you might not come back or even worse, something would happen to you. Jacc, you know I wouldn't send you on a blind mission. It's your call, buddy, how you want to play this."

Keith was right. I knew he wasn't trying to send me off. He was only reporting what was told to him. The question that still remained was how reliable was the information he was given? If it were some kind of prank, what would be the point of it? Who the hell knew? I didn't have time to ponder or figure it out. As Keith stated, Diane had been counting down the days for my return. I definitely didn't want to disappoint her.

"Keith, tell you what, I'll head over to Sheridan Park and see if Diane is there. You head to the other park and bring her back if she's waiting for me. If she's there, tell her I love her and I have some good news."

"Okay. I need to stop by my stash spot away. If Diane's there, I'll bring her right to you. If I don't see her, I'll head to Sheridan Park to make sure you guys finally hooked up."

"All right, thanks again, Keith. I've got so much to tell you guys, but it'll have to wait until later. Right now all I want to do is see Diane. I'd better get going. Talk with you later." Turning around, I began to head toward the main exit as Keith's voice filtered through the noisy room.

"Be careful, Jacc!"

"I will!" I yelled as I pressed my way through the crowd. Finally reaching the exit, I turned around to wave goodbye to Keith one last time, but he'd vanished into the crowd.

Stepping out into the bright sunny air, I briskly walked to the subway station and boarded the northbound train heading to Uptown. Finding a window seat, I aimless stared out of it. Barely paying attention to the scenery flashing by as the train rapidly zipped down its tracks, I let my mind fill up with thoughts of Diane and her reaction to everything I was going to tell her. Completely absorbed, I didn't even notice twenty minutes later that the train had pulled into the

Wilson stop.

Jumping up, I ran to the doors just as they were about to close. Glad I hadn't missed the stop, I raced down the platform stairs. Quickly glancing at an overhead clock in the train station as I walked out, I began strolling through the impoverished neighborhood. It was five after twelve. I knew Diane would at least wait thirty minutes for me. The grime of the littered filled streets could be seen everywhere as seedy characters lurked in the doorways and back alleys of rundown storefronts.

Deciding to take a shortcut, I trekked through a popular section of the area known as "Blood Alley." It was a section where drug selling, pimping, and all manner of prevalent criminal activity were upheld by the local undesirables.

That uneasy feeling came over me again when I turned on Broadway and began heading to Sheridan Park. I couldn't for the life of me figure out why Diane would want to meet in this neighborhood again? Finally reaching the park, I strolled through it looking for Diane. It was deserted. She definitely hadn't intended to meet me here. If she had, she'd already be here. I was pretty sure she was waiting for me at the other park. Thank God Keith had gone to meet her. They were probably on their way here right now.

Walking over to a bench, I sat down to wait for them. It was obvious Kango had lied to Keith, but why? The guy was probably high off of crack. The more I thought about it, the more ticked off I became. This was a complete waste of time.

"Hey, Jacc! I see you made it!" Standing up, I watched as Kango, Malcolm, and several other guys approached me.

"Kango, what the hell is going on? What's this all about?"

"You hear that, fellas?" Malcolm said as he walked right up and got in my face, his stale breath making me cringe.

"Jaccie, boy, wants to know what this is all about." Stepping back, he turned to Kango and tossed him a large bag of crack.

"Here, you earned it for a job well done. Tell Jacc all about our little deal." Gripping the crack firmly, Kango reluctantly shoved it into his pocket. He looked like all he wanted to do at that moment was go somewhere and light up his pipe. Glancing at me as if I were a sudden hindrance in his plans, he said, "Let's just get this over with. Jacc, it's like this. Malcolm feels he has a score to settle with you. He put the word out on the street if anyone can find you then he'll take care of them in a big way. It was just my good luck I ran into your buddy today. I knew all I had to do is let him think I'd seen Diane and he'd lead you right to us."

"That's right," Malcolm smirked. "We knew you'd come looking for her. Can't say I blame you. We all wanted to tap that ass for a long time. Just be glad we tricked you down here instead of her." Malcolm's comment about Diane ignited my anger. The mere thought of him or anyone of those vipers touching her made me sick. "If you ever harm Diane, I'll break your neck." Just as I was about to step toward

Malcolm, two guys grabbed me while the others surrounded me. A sinister gleam reflected in Malcolm eyes as he watched me struggle to free myself. "Malcolm, I would stick around, but I got things to do." Never taking his eyes off me, Malcolm nodded. "All right, Kango, go do what you gotta do." Eager to go, Kango ran off.

"Now back to you," Malcolm said as he once again got up in my face. "Whose fucking neck you gonna break?" Before I could even blink, he delivered a blow to my jaw causing blood to spew out as my teeth rattled when they hit the back of my mouth. "Still wanna talk shit?" Before I could recover, he hit me again. "I told you if I ever caught you on the streets, your ass is mine. I guess today is my lucky day." Rippling pain shot through my head as the sting of his blows lit up my entire face. Enraged, I fought to break free of the hold on me. Yanking and pulling, I finally broke loose and kicked Malcolm in his balls. "Oh shit!!!!!!" he yelled as he doubled over in pain. "Get that mutha-fucka, now!"

Although I was outnumbered, my quick reflexes helped me fight off several of the guys before they eventually encircled me. Everything began to move fast from that point. One minute I was standing in the circle, assessing my opponents as I calculated my next move, the next moment I was lying on the ground as they moved in on me like a pack of wolves. Curled up, I tried to shield myself as best I could. Punches and kicks were coming from everywhere. Not sure how long I endured the brutal beating, I vaguely remembered praying someone would come along and stop them before they killed me. I was a bloody mess. Excruciating pain shot through my entire body. My face was almost unrecognizable as blows continued to pound it, leaving me practically punch drunk.

Finally the blows became less and less as the beating started to ease up and the circle widened to let Malcolm through. Barely able to lift my head, I struggled to see what was going on. One of my eyes was swollen shut. Through a blurry haze, I saw Malcolm point a gun at me as he stood over me. His eyes blazed with raw hatred. They were void of any human compassion as he pulled back the trigger.

"I said you wouldn't live to see your next birthday and I was right. You're a dead man." Popping off several shots, Malcolm spat on me as one final act of cruelty. Reaching down, he fumbled through my pockets, in search of my wallet. Not able to find it, he took my cell phone and ran off with the crowd.

The painful sting of the bullets entering my body was nothing like I'd ever experienced. Not able to move, my head began to fill with images of Diane as I lay in a pool of blood. I prayed she and Keith would make it in time to get me to a hospital. I fought to hang on.

"Hey, Diane! Come on, Jacc's waiting for us!"

"Jacc? Where is he? Keith, I don't understand. Is everything all right?"

"That remains to be seen. Come on, we don't have

time to waste. I'll tell you all about it on the way. Here, let me have your backpack. If we hurry, we can catch that bus across the street."

"Geez, that was close, Keith."

"Yes, it was, Diane, but we made it. Come on, I see two seats toward the back of the bus."

"All right, now that we're sitting, are you going to tell me what's going on?"

"I'm not sure what's going on, Diane. All I know is earlier Kango told me you wanted to get word to Jacc about meeting you at Sheridan Park. I found Jacc at Union Station and told him your location had been changed."

"Kango lied. I haven't seen or talked to him since we left Uptown. Even if I had run into him, why would I trust him with important information as to where I was planning on meeting Jacc? It's none of his damn business."

"I agree. Both Jacc and I thought the whole thing sounded kind of suspicious, but we didn't want to take a chance and have you miss each other. He went to Sheridan Park to see if you were there and he sent me to see if you were here you just in case the whole thing was bogus."

'You're damn right this whole thing is bogus. I don't like this at all. Kango can't be trusted. He's definitely up to something. We should have taken the subway. This bus is moving way too slow."

"Yeah, I know. I'm just as anxious to get there as you are. The sooner we meet up with Jacc, the better. You guys can have your reunion and then I say we all get the hell out of Uptown. Oh, by the way, he told me to tell you he loved you and he had some good news. "

"Keith, I can't wait to see him. As far as I'm concerned, knowing Jacc made it back and he's waiting for me is good news. Come on, this is our stop. Let's hurry up and find him."

"Hey, wait up!"

"Thanks for waiting."

"Was somebody chasing you?"

"No."

"Then why in the world were you hollering down the street like an idiot and running as if the devil himself were after you?"

"I wanted to walk with you."

"Is that all?"

"No, that's not all. I wanted to introduce myself. I'm Ja—"

"I know who you are."

"You do?"

"What?"

"You're a strange one, Jacc "Don't you know being on the trail and especially in this community, everyone gets to know who everyone is? Of course I know who you are,

silly. And I'm sure you know who I am."

"Yeah, I guess you're right, Diane."

"Jacc! Jacc! Wake up, Jacc!"

"Wh-what's wrong. What's going on?"

"Man, something's going down in the women's dorm. I hear it's really bad."

"Excuse me! Let me through! Let me through, damn it! Oh...my...God! Diane!"

"Whhhhyyyyy...wwwhhhhhhy? My God, whhhhhhyyyy?"

"Who the hell did this? Answer me! I want to know what low life did this to hhhhherrrrrrrrr!!!"

"Drop out of school and you won't receive another dime from me. Do you hear me, Jacc? I mean it. I'll cut you off so fast; you won't know what hit you!"

"Jacc, come back here! We're not through! If you walk out that door, that's it. I wash my hands of you! Jacc! Jacc! Jaaaaaaccccc!"

"Man, you don't know who you're fucking with. I'll beat you down like a bitch on the street. Get up out of my chair!"

"Malcolm, show him you ain't no punk. Hit the white faggot and floor his ass!"

"J-Jacc, is it really you?"

"Yeah, David, it's really me."

"My God, you've come home."

"I'm here to see if we could put the past behind us and work on being a family. I've wanted to come home for a long time, but I was afraid you'd reject me."

"Reject you? Jacc, you rejected us. You're the one who decided to leave, remember?"

"I came back to ask if you can float me a loan. I just need enough to invest in a project I've been contemplating."

"Jacc, you don't need me to float you any money. Hell, you have enough money to do whatever you want to do. You're a rich man, Jacc."

"Wh-whaat?"

"I-I don't understand, David. You're joking, because if you're not, then what the hell are you talking about?"

"Jacc, I'm serious. You're filthy rich. I know you think dad cut you out of the will, but he didn't. He left the bulk of his fortune to you and me."

"Jacc, darling, don't be angry at your father. He didn't mean what he said."

"Mom, dad hates me. He thinks I'm a loser."

"J-Jacc, I don't have much time. Y-Y-You have to accept the fact that I'm dying. You have to let go."

"No, Mom, don't say that. I won't let you die. You can't die. You're all I have."

"Mom, Mom, Mom! Oh, God, no! Mommmm!!!!!"

It's true what they say about your entire life flashing before you when death stares you in the face. Not really sure how long I'd been lying there, the events of my life rapidly spiraled out of sequence as voices suddenly echoed all around me. Feeling extremely weak, I fought to make sense of everything, but the images were blurry as I continued to slip in and out of consciousness. Presently I was barely conscious as I mustered all my strength to hold on just a little longer. I wanted to see and hear Diane one last time. I wanted to tell her how much I loved her and let her know that everything was going to be all right. They might succeed in taking my life, but they weren't going to get the victory by killing the dream. I had to hang on a little while longer. If only God would allow me just a little more time. I had to talk to her one last time.

"Jacc! Jacc! Where are you?" Not sure if I were still hearing imaginary voices, I began to focus on the faint sounds traveling through the wind. "Jacccc! Jaccc! Look, Keith, there's someone lying over there!" Recognizing Diane's voice, I tried to get up, but the crippling pain was too much. A tear rolled down my cheek as I thanked God for allowing me another chance to see her.

"Dear God, Jacc, you're hurt!" she cried once she reached me. Dropping to the ground, she flung her arms around me and sobbed. "Oh, God, please let him be all right." Rocking back and forth, she cradled my head in her arms as tears streamed down her face. "Keith, do something! He's lost a lot of blood! I think he's been shot! Go get help!"

"Damn those bastards for doing this to you! Hang in there, Jacc. You're gonna be all right. I'm gonna go get help right away!" Tears welled in Keith's eyes as he ran off.

Mustering up every bit of strength I had, I squeezed her hand. "D-D-Diane, I-I love you. I'm so sorry t-t-this has t-t-turned out this way."

"Oh, Jacc," she sobbed, "Please don't try and talk. You need to preserve your strength. You've got to hold on, baby. Help is on the way." A sense of urgency suddenly came over me. There was so much I needed to say to her before it was too late. I could feel myself growing weaker and weaker.

"D-D-Diane, listen to me. W-w-we don't have much time."

"No, Jacc, don't say that. You're going to be all right. You came back to me. I waited for you and you came back to me. You have to believe you're going to make it!" The denial in Diane's voice mingled with the overwhelming sadness in her eyes momentarily took me back to the day my mother lay dying in the hospital. Just like Diane, I too didn't want to accept what was happening. I would have fought the devil himself to save my mother as Diane was ready to fight the good battle of faith for me. Somehow I had to make her listen because I knew time was running out. For whatever reason, God was calling me home. "D-Diane, p-please, listen to me. I don't want you to be sad. Everything is going to change for the better in your life. My w-wallet is inside my p-p-pocket. There's a business card inside the wallet with my brother's phone number on it. Get the number and promise me you'll call David. He'll know what to do."

"Jacc, I—"

"Diane, p-p-please get the number, now!" With shaky hands, she fumbled inside my pocket. "I got it," she said as she pulled out the card from the wallet. Feeling extremely relieved, I knew she was going to be all right once she spoke with my brother. "Promise me you'll call David, promise me, Diane."

"I promise, Jacc, I'll call your brother. Please don't talk anymore. You have to save all your strength. Where the hell is Keith with the help?" she cried out in frustration. Extremely weak, I knew my time was at hand. "D-D-Diane, I'm not going to make it."

"Stop it! Stop it, Jacc! Don't say that!"

"It's true. Don't be sad. I love you. I'll never stop loving you."

"Nooo! You can't die on me, Jacc. You can't, die. I won't let you. I love you. Please don't leave me. You have to fight and hold on! " It was too late. There was no more fight left in me. I was fading fast. "Diane," I uttered as I took my last breath, "I love you."

"NNNNNOOOOOOOOO!" Diane wailed "Dear God, NNNOOOOOOOOOO!"

"Over here, officer! They're right over here!" Keith along with the paramedics and several police officers rushed up to Diane. "Diane, how is he?" She turned to him. "He's dead, Keith! He's dead! Those low down bastards killed him. Damn them all to hell! Sobs rippled through her body as fresh tears broke like a damn and she cried uncontrollably. Bending down, the paramedics checked for my pause before they covered my body and took me way. Helping Diane up, Keith held her as she cried. "I'm so sorry, Diane. I'm so sorry." His own eyes filled with tears as he realized he'd lost his best friend. His grief was just as profound as hers.

TRUE LOVE

For Those Who've Experienced True Love

True Love doesn't leave room for doubt

True Love causes you to joyfully shout

True Love is compassionate and understanding

True Love is never rude or too demanding

True Love isn't weighed down with fear

True Love embraces you and wipes away your tear

True Love wants to shield and protect

True Love will never show disrespect

True Love doesn't cheat, plot, or scheme

True Love is like living a romantic dream

True Love doesn't tear you down, but it builds you up

True Love is breaking bread, sharing the wine, and your sup

True Love is togetherness holding hands

True Love is definitely part of God's divine plan

– Diane –

*C*hapter Twelve ✍

One week later –

"WE STAND here today in the hope and glory of the rebirth into eternal life through Our Lord and Savior, Jesus Christ as we hand over to Almighty God our brother, Jaccson Ford. We entrust his body into the ground. From the earth he came and to the earth he returns. May the Lord bless him, keep him, and let his face to shine on him as he rests in peace. Amen."

"Thank you, Reverend Brown for the lovely service. This is a beautiful cemetery."

"You're welcome, my child. I'm sure Jacc's soul is at peace. I'd like to introduce his brother, David."

"Hi, Diane, It's good to finally meet you after our telephone conversation."

"Yes it is, David. I'm glad to finally meet you too."

"I'll leave you two alone. You probably have a lot to talk about."

"All right, Reverend. And thanks again."

"Diane, would you like to sit down? There's a bench over there."

"Sure, why not? It feels good to sit. I'm glad it didn't rain. It seems like it rains every time I attend a funeral."

"Diane, there's something very important I want to discuss with you."

"Yes, I know. Before Jacc died, he asked me…in fact…he made me promise to call you. He said you'd know what to do. I'm not exactly sure what he meant, but I suspect he thought you could make a dream he once told me about become a reality. Your brother was the most compassionate person I'd ever known. He wanted to end homelessness by building homes for the homeless. It's a beautiful concept, but it takes major dollars to do that. I don't know why Jacc thought you could help. I doubt seriously if you can."

"Diane, Jacc told me about his dream when he came to visit me."

"When he came to visit you? When was this?"

"Two weeks ago. He came home after reading about our father's passing. He told me an amazing story about a woman he'd met who was kind and caring, a woman who knew firsthand the evil that lurked behind shelter doors. He told me this woman shared his vision to help the homeless. I can see why he fell in love with you. You're a beautiful and obvious intelligent woman. From what Jacc told me, you have the same selfless nature that he had."

"You're right. I think our desire to help others is what brought us together. We used to have philosophical discussions about ending homelessness, but as I said it was just talk."

"Diane, I'm not sure what Jacc told you about our father. He was a very wealthy man. Jacc and my father often butted heads. Dad was always pushing Jacc to go into the family business. I guess I might have been guilty of that as well. Jacc was never really interested in filling dad's or my shoes. Being a free spirit, he just wasn't comfortable in the corporate world. Dad didn't approve at all. He always felt Jacc could have done a lot better if he'd applied himself. Things came to blows a few years after our mother loss her ongoing battle with cancer. Jacc came home one afternoon and announced he was dropping out of college. Dad hit the roof. They ended up in the worst shouting match I'd ever heard. Dad ultimately told Jacc he'd cut him off financially as well as cut him out of his will. Not giving a damn about the money, Jacc told dad where to get off before he stormed out. That was thirteen years ago. Jacc basically disappeared. No one knew where he was. He hasn't been seen or heard from in thirteen years, that is, until he finally came home two weeks ago after reading in a newspaper that our dad had died a month ago."

"My God, David, I never knew. Jacc didn't go into great detail about his family. He did mention once he had a father and a younger brother, but that was the extent of it. No wonder he was acting kind of strange the night before he decided to leave. I saw him reading something in an old newspaper, but he wouldn't let me see read it. Whatever it was, he was literally shaken. When I questioned him about it, he just changed the subject. The next morning he announced he was leaving. I was very upset. I didn't understand what would prompt him to want to take off like that. He said he'd explain everything when he returned in two weeks. We were supposed to meet two weeks from the day he left as I explained to you in our phone conversation, but as you know, things didn't turn out how we'd planned. It's all so sad, the situation with Jacc's father and learning about his death, not to mention Jacc's senseless death. It's just so cruel."

"Diane, I know. I'm just as heartbroken over Jacc's death. We'd grown close during the past two weeks. The time we spent together brought us closer than we'd ever been before. We were able to make peace with ourselves and Jacc was finally able to have closure and peace with our father. For years Jacc thought dad never loved him, but it's not true. Our father loved Jacc more than he ever really outwardly showed. Dad spent countless years searching for him. Despite what was said during that heated argument between them, dad left the bulk of his wealth to both Jacc and I when he died. Jacc's coming back was partially due to you and his vision. I was totally shocked when Jacc came home after thirteen years. When I told him dad hadn't cut him out of his will, he told me all about his vision. Jacc also made me promise to give you this if something should ever happen to him."

"What's this?" She stared at the envelope David had placed in her hand. Opening it, she read its contents.

My dearest Diane, if you're reading this letter then

I'm probably already dead. First, and foremost, I want you to know that I've never known a love like ours. I truly thank God he placed you in my life's path. I love you, sweet, Diane, and I don't want you to ever again suffer from a lack of money. I'm leaving you all that I've inherited. You'll find in the envelope a notarized copy of my last will and testament. You're the sole beneficiary of my estate, a net worth of 2.2 billion dollars. Diane, know that our love will never die. As long as you keep me in your heart, I'll always be near you. You can now live our dream and be a blessing to those who find themselves walking down the homeless trail. Love, Jacc.

The shock of what she'd just read was overwhelming. Tears flowed down her cheeks as she placed the letter on her lap. "Oh...my...God...David...he left me 2.2 billion dollars!"

"That's right. He knew you'd use the money for the betterment of humanity. It was his intention to help the homeless. He felt the money was a gift from God."

"David, you can rest assure the money is going to be used to make Jacc's dream become a reality. He was the love of my life. Even in his death, he taught us charity's greatest gift comes from the heart. His generous gift is going to bless a lot of people. I'm going to dedicate the rest of my life to making sure it does."

❦❦❦❦❦

LIGHTS...CAMERA...ACTION!

Celebrating Life Through The Eyes Of The Reel

Life is like a groovy movie
Whether guy or chick
You're the star of your wonderful flick
Surrounded by your supporting cast
Strive to make your movie last
For those climatic scenes
There's a purpose to everything
You're the director of your show
With the power to say who'll come and go
Treat the villains like the extras they are
With no real success of getting far
As they appear in their cameo shot
Remember their purpose is to add to the plot
When the credits finally end your film
And the heavenly Oscars are given out
Know you definitely have cause to shout
Whether guy or chick
You were the star in your wonderful flick

– Jacc –

*E*pilogue ✍

Croydon, London, June, 2026 –

STANDING at the glass podium in the crowded banquet hall, Diane took a deep breath as she looked out over the massive crowd. "Good evening, ladies and gentlemen. I want to thank you for coming out to support our founder's day dinner. Today will mark the twenty-fifth anniversary of The Jacc Ford Foundation. As you know the foundation is named in honor of Jaccson Ford. Affectionately known as Jacc, Mr. Ford was the eldest son of the late business tycoon Charles H. Ford. Jacc was also a compassionate visionary with a heart of gold and a dear, personal, friend of mine. Thanks to his generous gift, The Jacc Ford Foundation has made it possible for homeless men and women around the world to rise above their personal crisis and become homeowners." The room resounded with applause. Glancing around, she took a moment before continuing.

"Twenty-five years ago, the foundation formed an alliance with Charles Ford Builders to offer a cost effective solution to the homeless crisis. Since then we've emerged as the forerunner in building affordable homes. We sale them for a mere $20,000 regardless of property size, market value, and cost for materials. The effective price ceiling was created as a way to make the homes affordable. To qualify for the homes our buyers must be homeless and agree to participate in our two-year program where they live rent-free in a temporary apartment. Our program is structured very different from the usual social service programs. We don't offer the traditional case management that most social services do. Why? Because we don't feel the need to police or control the lives of our participants nor do we feel that they need to be rehabilitated or reformed in any shape or form."

Diane paused for a moment to gather her thoughts. All eyes were on her when she continued. "There are so many social agencies out there that are primarily focusing on fixing the social ills of the homeless through either subliminal punishment or by misclassifying them instead of seeing the situation for what it really is. Homelessness stems from poverty and a lack of affordable housing. The social ills of the homeless are the same social ills that the entire world encounters. If anything, homelessness is the manifestation of the individual's economic crisis not the cause of it. We strongly believe that whether a substance abuser or not, whether mentality ill or not, every impoverished person deserves a chance to live independently in decent affordable housing."

"This is why our temporary apartments are structured for independent living where the tenants govern and oversee their own lives. We don't have case managers making visits to their apartments. We don't regulate their visitors or guests. There are no curfews or group activities or meetings they have to attend. We designed our program this way to disband the structure of homeless individuals having to subject themselves to institutionalized living via social programs and their subsidized housing. So in a essence, they live as freely and as independently as you and I, except all of their housing expenses are being paid for via the Jacc Ford Foundation during the two or three years that they are in the program."

"The apartment buildings are multi units that are owned by the foundation. We fit the bill for utilities, water, and the upkeep of the buildings along with furniture vouchers for their apartments. What the tenants are responsible for is their own food, transportation expenses, and other amenities they may feel they need or want. The only requirements that we impose on them is that they open up a saving account and show us monthly statements proving that they are saving their money so they'll be able to purchase our homes in a two year span."

As Diane's eyes scanned the audience, she paused to take a sip of water. She could see she had everyone's attention. "In two years, if they aren't able to save $20,000, they're given a year's extension to save it. All participants must have some sort of income whether it's through work or disability. By entering our program, participants who are not working yet don't qualify for disability must agree to actively look for work. We give them a grace period of six months to find employment. For those who would prefer to have some sort of involvement with a case manager, we do network with social agencies and can provide referrals to the tenants who would like to seek out job counseling, treatment for any substance abuse, or counseling for mental health issues."

"Let me just say our mission isn't to continuously provide free living, but to allow enough time for the participants to successfully save their money and purchase their own homes. The purpose of the program is to motivate them to become homeowners by giving them an incentive verses remaining codependent on modern day plantations known as shelters or subsided apartments funded, controlled, and run by social agencies. We've found in the long run it's more beneficial for people to own their own home verses continuing to struggle to pay monthly rent. Once they finish the program, we sell them a home according to their family size. We're an international nonprofit organization. All money obtained from the sell of our homes is reinvested back into building other homes."

"What we've virtually done is provide an avenue for impoverished people to finally liberate themselves from the cycle of homelessness. We've made it possible for them to obtain their dream of being homeowners along with easing their burden of trying to pay off a 30 year mortgage and eliminating the risk of them losing their home through foreclosure if they can't make the monthly payments. Homelessness in America has dropped by eighty-five percent since we first opened our doors. We've successfully housed several million families. Our aim is to completely eliminate homelessness not only in the US, but internationally as well."

Motioning for someone to dim the lights, Diane turned around and glanced up. "If you look at the overhead, you'll see what I affectionately call *The House That Jacc Built*." Sounds of amazement could be heard throughout the room as the crowd stared at the big screen. Depicted were Daryl and Clarice standing in front of a beautiful home of magnificent style and design. Several other beautiful homes were also shown with their owners.

"As you see, all our homes are professionally built. We spared no expense and we used only top quality material provided by Charles Ford Builders. It was Jacc's dream to build beautiful homes for the homeless. Even in his untimely death, he visualized this day. Although he didn't live long enough to see his dream materialize, I'm certain Jacc would be proud to know his vision has touched the lives of millions. Just as I'm also sure he's smiling down on us from heaven. On that note, I say let the celebration begin. I hope you enjoy tonight's festivities."

Diane was right. I was smiling down on her as I watched her celebrate another successful year as president of The Jacc Ford Foundation. Although I missed her, I knew her journey on earth was far from over. It wouldn't be over until every homeless person finally had a place they could truly call home. There were many more houses to build and many more families to enjoy them. I also knew my dream would continue to live on through Diane…the woman I love…the woman I left behind. This would forever be our story.

THE FABRIC OF OUR LIVES

Embroidered In God's Perfect Love

The Fabric of Our Lives is sown together by a common
Thread
That coils around the spool of God's Head

The Fabric of Our Lives is patterned after his Holy Plan
And distributed throughout the entire Land
The Fabric of Our Lives is weaved in mercy and in Love
It's modeled by the angels far Above

The Fabric of Our Lives is fashioned for all to See
It's rooted in the ground like an old Oak Tree
The Fabric of Our Lives stitches our Story
Detailing our happiness, pain, and our Glory

The Fabric of our Lives is about you and Me
Where we've been, where we're going, and our ultimate
Destiny

−Jacc & Diane −

About The Author

Dawn Walker a native of Chicago, Illinois, majored in communications while in college. Other books by Ms. Walker are **The Protector** and **Love's Silent Storm** and **CeBreeze.** Besides writing, she enjoys reading, drawing, and doing word search puzzles.

To learn more about the author visit:

www.readmybooks.org